Date Due

The Adventures of
RAMA

The Story of the Great Hindu Epic Ramayana

The Adventures of

Rama

by

JOSEPH GAER

Illustrated by Randy Monk

LITTLE, BROWN AND COMPANY · BOSTON

Published simultaneously in Canada
by Little, Brown & Company (Canada) Limited

PRINTED IN THE UNITED STATES OF AMERICA

Introduction

Ancient Greece produced an enduring literature; and towering among the Greek literary works are two epics: the Iliad and the Odyssey. Ancient India, too, produced a great literature; and like two spires above the massive Hindu classics rise their epic poems: the Ramayana and the Mahabharata.

While the Greek epics are widely known to us, the Hindu epics are strange to us even by name. Yet they present a more complete description of an early civilization than may be found in any other early record. More important, they are unsurpassed in any literature as richly inventive and stirring tales.

The first of these Hindu epics, the Ramayana (which means The Adventures of Rama), bears a resemblance to the Greek Iliad, and has often been called the Indian Iliad, because of the similarity in the main outlines of the important events. But to the Hindus, who have kept this epic alive in their hearts and imagination for so many centuries, it is more than a great poem dealing with the adventures of Prince Rama. It is part of their Sacred Scriptures. For to them it is the story of their god, Vishnu the Preserver, who came in the mortal form of Prince Rama to save mankind from evil as represented in the Ruler of the Giants, King Ravan.

What kept this epic so fresh in the hearts of successive generations, however, is the fact that it is primarily a superlative love story, which the Hindus cherish — just as we cherish the great love stories of Romeo and Juliet, Tristan and Isolde, Lancelot and Guinevere, or the poet Dante and Beatrice. But unlike other love stories in world literature, the Ramayana is interwoven into an historic record of great antiquity. In it an alliance is portrayed of certain northern tribes and primitive aborigines of central India who, together, set out to conquer and subdue the barbarian tribes of the south, all the way to Ceylon. In the folk imagination, these events of an early Golden Age flowered into a magnificent recital in which gods and demons, as mortals, touched the lofty heights of love and loyalty and the depths of duplicity and vengeance.

For centuries the adventures of Prince Rama and Princess Sita in that Golden Age were preserved by word of mouth. The people learned it in their youth and then taught it to the generation following. And each generation reverently added to the recital its own

embroidery. Bards and storytellers arose who special-
ized in reciting the Adventures of Rama. Parts of the
very long epic were chanted to the accompaniment
of music at every conceivable anniversary of living.
In time people came to regard the mere reciting of
the story, or parts of it, as having the power to cure
disease, absolve people from sin, bring happiness to
the sorrowful, and transport the dying into the
Heaven of Vishnu.

About five centuries before the Christian era, a
poet named Valmiki gathered the many legends and
stories about Prince Rama and Princess Sita and wove
them into a unified epic written in Sanskrit. Since
printing was unknown for many centuries after Valmiki's time, his poem was preserved by copyists. But,
as in the case of most early written works that survived the centuries, the copyists did not merely copy.
They added much of their own. And it is often hard
to tell which is the original and which the added material.

In the sixteenth century a Brahman poet named
Tulsi-Das (1532–1623) rendered the Ramayana into
Hindi, one of the modern languages of Upper India.
Inspired by the Christian Gospels, he transformed the
valiant Prince Rama into a savior who came in mortal
form to bring salvation to mankind. The Tulsi-Das

version gained widespread popularity but it did not supersede the original Valmiki version.

In this book the Valmiki version of the Ramayana is followed.

The Ramayana by Valmiki is overwhelmingly long. It consists of seven books, divided into five hundred cantos, containing twenty-four thousand stanzas. The poem is lush with descriptions of nature, miraculous deeds, great battles, strange rites and customs, feasts and revelries, intrigues between mortals and gods, exultations and lamentations, and astounding portrayals of human beings in conflict.

The task of reducing so huge and so complex a work to a prose story the length of this book might be likened to an attempt to reduce a vast mural painting to a page-sized sketch in black and white. Nevertheless, this book attempts to retain the flavor of this stirring epic and "to bring perhaps from afar what is already founded," as Walt Whitman puts it. Many episodes — rites, genealogies, miraculous events, feasts, legends — which digress from the main story line were completely omitted. Otherwise the Valmiki version of the Ramayana was followed, book by book.

Contents

CONTENTS

Acknowledgments

Foremost among those to whom I am indebted are the many scholars who, in the past century, have opened up to the Western world India's literary treasury of the great epics, delectable fables and inimitable poetry. Since neither Sanskrit nor Prakrit or Hindi or Pali are known to me, in the preparation of this book I depended entirely on the several translations of the Ramayana and the Ramacaritamanasa; and more particularly the Ramayana by Valmiki, rendered into English verse almost in its entirety, over eighty years ago, by Ralph T. H. Griffith.

For their perceptive reactions and valuable suggestions on the manuscript of the book, I gratefully acknowledge my indebtedness to: Professor Wayland D. Hand, folklorist at the University of California in Los Angeles; Professor Malcolm Pitt, Department of Indian Studies, Hartford Seminary Foundation; Dr. M. O. Thomas, Hartford Theological Seminary; Swami Aseshananda of the Vedanta Society of Southern California; Rosemary Livsey, Director of Work with Children, Los Angeles Public Library; and Ruth Robinson, Children's Librarian, Westchester Branch, Los Angeles Public Library.

J.G.

The Adventures of
RAMA

After all not to create only, or found only,
But to bring perhaps from afar what is already
                                              founded,
To give it our own identity, average, limitless, free,
To fill the gross the torpid bulk with vital religious
                                                  fire,
Not to repel or destroy so much as accept, fuse, re-
                                          habilitate,
To obey as well as to command, to follow more than
                                          to lead,
These also are the lessons of the New World;
While how little the New after all, how much the
                                  Old, Old World!

from WALT WHITMAN,
SONG OF THE EXPOSITION

I

Rama's Youth

(Bala-kanda)

Children of the Sun

ON THE BANKS of the Sagara River, at the foot of
the Himalaya Mountains, a thousand times a thousand
years ago, there lived the prosperous nation known
as the Kosalas: Children of the Sun. Their land was
fertile and their wealth in cattle and grain and gold
passed all reckoning.

In the center of this fortunate kingdom rose the
royal city, Ayodhya. According to legend, Ayodhya
was designed by Manu, the Father of Mankind. The
city measured sixty miles in length and fifteen miles
in width, and was encircled by great walls inlaid
with richly decorated crests and shields of the Kosala
nobles. Below the high ramparts, deep and wide
moats reminded any envious foe that the name Ayodhya meant The Invincible City.

Within the city, the streets were wide as royal
highways, and down their length flowed limpid
streams to cool the summer air; and on both sides of

3

the sweet waters grew flowering trees of great age and rare beauty. Each home was like a castle and rose from the mango groves, the terraced gardens and the lily-covered pools that surrounded it.

Fairer than the city were the inhabitants of Ayodhya: the men broad-shouldered and handsome, the women comely and full of grace. Besides their wealth in worldly treasures, the people were rich in wit and wisdom; in the gift of song and speech; in lore and learning; and in the love of their neighbors. The only poor amongst them were the sages who, of their own free will, had taken the vow of poverty and put on the yellow robe of the priestly beggar. These were accorded great reverence, and none were allowed to suffer need.

Through the gates of Ayodhya came and went a constant stream of royal elephants and fiery steeds bearing envoys sent by distant kings; merchants bringing precious wares on carts or litters; bards and ballad singers, holy men and artisans on foot. Ayodhya, famed for its beauty and the goodness of its people, attracted the wise and learned from all realms; and they came to visit the place where lying and deceit were unknown, and where crime was as alien as despair.

In this joyful city, in a palace of surpassing splendor, lived King Dasaratha, the far-famed ruler of the

Children of the Sun. The people loved their aged king; and the king loved his people. And they all took pride in his four young sons, Rama, Lakshman, Satrughna and Bharat.

When the princes were old enough, they were entrusted to carefully chosen teachers for their training. The royal brothers distinguished themselves early in nimbleness of mind, in sharpness of eye, and in dexterity of hand. They could send arrows through the air with great skill; they could unfalteringly recite the Holy Scripts; and each could take full command of a spirited elephant.

Most skillful of the four was the oldest prince, named Rama, which means The Great Delight.

From early childhood Prince Rama favored his half brother, Lakshman; and Lakshman worshiped Rama. He would not sit down until Rama was seated; he would not eat unless Rama ate also; and whatever Rama did, Lakshman tried to do, to please his older brother.

Just as Lakshman loved Rama, so did his twin brother, Prince Satrughna, love his half brother, Bharat. The princes always paired off: Rama with Lakshman; Bharat with Satrughna.

Between them was no jealousy, no rivalry, no desire on the part of any of them to excel the others. Yet, whether in archery or chariot racing, in sacred

5

rites or elephant training, Rama, being the oldest, was accepted as the leader.

By the time Prince Rama reached his sixteenth birthday, he was tall, broad-shouldered, strong of limb, with all parts of his body divinely proportioned. His bluish-black skin was lustrous and soft as velvet; and his eyes, large and dark, shone as if lighted from within. By nature wise, he sought to learn from the wise. The people of the Kosala kingdom compared their Prince Rama to the Lord of the Moon. Prince Rama, they said, was as patient as Mother Earth; but when aroused in anger he was fiercer than the World-Destroying Fire.

King Dasaratha proudly began to call upon his oldest son to join in the assembly of the royal councilors to learn the problems that arose within the realm. And though Rama remained silent in the presence of his elders, when they asked for his opinion, he spoke wisely, and on the side of justice. Soon the elders of the Children of the Sun began to favor Rama's thoughts in their decisions.

Request of a Sage

One day the deliberations of the Royal Council were interrupted by a guard announcing that the most honored sage in all the land, Vishvamitra, was at the gate and asked for an audience with the king. King Dasaratha arose at once and hastened to welcome the holy man.

"Your visit, O honored guest," said the king, "is as welcome as rain to ground long parched by drought. With all my heart I welcome you! Make known what brings you here, and even before you utter your wish I vow it shall be granted you!"

Vishvamitra replied: "I shall tell you instantly what brings me here: Two powerful demons, who can change their forms at will, disturb me at the sacred rites, desecrate my sacrifices, and turn all my contemplation into confusion. The demons know I cannot banish them with a curse because no threatening word can be uttered at the holy rites. O warrior of the warrior caste, I have come to you for help!"

"Command me!" said the king.

"O Lion among Men!" said the sage. "I beseech you to send your son, Rama, to destroy the demons; and I shall bless him for his deeds!"

King Dasaratha paled and his hands began to tremble. He opened his mouth to speak, but no words came. His eyes grew misty and he heard the sound of distant bells as he crumpled in his seat.

After attendants had revived him, the monarch pleaded with the sage: "O honored guest! My son is but a child! What can a youth do against fiends whose strength and skill and magic arts no mortal weapon can defeat? I fear for my son, who is dearer to me than my own life. Ask for anything else — ask that I myself shall engage these powerful demons in battle — but do not ask for Rama!"

Vishvamitra rose in anger and spoke his displeasure: "A king's promise must never be broken! Nor should you fear for Rama. For by my merit in the eyes of the gods in heaven, I promise that neither man nor demon shall do him harm. For I shall teach Prince Rama the use of weapons so mighty that none shall ever be able to defeat him."

The king sighed in resignation and sent an attendant to summon Rama.

Prince Rama appeared with his half brother Lakshman close behind him. And when the king explained Vishvamitra's request, Rama bowed and said:

"The Brahman does his duty when he performs the holy rites; and it is the duty of our warrior caste to protect him in fulfilling it."

Lakshman at once pleaded with his father for permission to accompany Rama; and the king consented.

King Dasaratha recited the Peace Chant; the priests chanted their benediction; and the mothers of

Rama and Lakshman, Kausalya the Good and Sumitra the Sweet, came to take leave of their sons.

To the sound of drums, Rama and Lakshman left the palace, following closely in the footsteps of the old sage, Vishvamitra.

The Lesson

When the royal brothers and the old man reached the banks of the Sarayu River, nine miles from the city, Vishvamitra said:

"Let us pause here and purify our bodies with water. Then, Prince Rama, I shall teach you the meaning of *Bala* and *Atibala*."

They bathed and then sat down upon the ground to refresh themselves with fruit. And after they had eaten, the old sage said:

"*Bala* and *Atibala* are two mystic doctrines, one mighty and the other mightier still. Knowing these, you will never suffer from hunger or thirst, from heat or cold, from illness or fatigue. And they shall make you invincible to all enemies."

"What if the enemy is also versed in *Bala* and *Atibala?*" asked Rama.

The sage shook his head and answered: "It is given to few to receive these two doctrines, which are Daughters of Brahma the Creator. You, my Prince,

9

have been chosen by destiny; for you are destined to wage great battles to cleanse the world of evil."

Rama bowed his head and reverently raised his hands, palm to palm. "I am your humble pupil, Great Sage!"

In words as bright as rays of light Vishvamitra explained to Rama the mystic doctrines of *Bala* and *Atibala*. By the time he had finished the great lesson, the sage grew very tired and fell asleep. The princes did not wish to disturb him and sat quietly, until they, too, were deep in dreamless sleep.

Next morning, before the sun was bright on the horizon, the old man wakened the sleeping youths, eager to start out upon the journey before the rising heat of day. And along their way the sage explained to Rama the meaning of charmed powers and their proper use, until they reached at last an ancient hermitage.

"Whose hermitage is that?" asked Lakshman.

Vishvamitra, as full of lore as a pomegranate is of seeds, related fact and legend about each place they passed; and of some, as of this ancient hermitage, his recollections went back far, to the beginning of time when gods and goddesses walked upon the earth. The hours passed quickly in the telling of his stories, consuming the day, and bringing another night for sleep upon the ground.

Rama and Lakshman followed the nimble old man for three days, and on the fourth day they reached Vishvamitra's hermitage.

The kindly sage enthralled them with his stories and wisdom, and Rama listened attentively to all his mystic teachings. Vishvamitra bestowed upon Rama wondrous weapons, one by one, and with each he taught the prince the sacred formula to be employed. Each weapon was capable of subduing a different kind of enemy, and of inflicting a different kind of pain. These varied weapons could not only wound and kill; they could throw fear into an enemy; or make him lose the will to fight; or so confuse him that he would be unable to defend himself.

After Vishvamitra had patiently taught his young pupil the use of all the weapons, the old man took his place before the altar to offer up a sacrifice. And at once a group of evil spirits descended to disrupt the sacred service.

Rama was prepared. He chose his weapons carefully; he uttered the sacred formulas precisely as they had been taught to him; and with their mystic power he quickly vanquished the disrupting spirits that had plagued the holy man.

When the last demon had been slain, Rama said to the sage: "The pledge my father gave you is fulfilled; and the lesson you have taught me is confirmed. Bless us, O Sage! And permit my brother and myself to return home, for our aged father anxiously awaits us."

"Stay this one night with me," said Vishvamitra, "and in the morning I shall bless you and send you on your way."

Contest for a Princess

Early next morning a disciple came to Vishvamitra's hermitage with word from the kingdom of Mithila:

King Janaka had announced a contest for the hand of his daughter, Princess Sita, known for her beauty in all the Seven Islands of the Earth.

"I must go to Mithila for the sacrifices preceding the king's contest," said Vishvamitra. "And it is my wish that you, Rama and Lakshman, come with me to take part in it."

The princes eagerly replied: "Your wish is our command."

That day the sage and the two youths started northward toward the banks of the Ganges on the slopes of the Himalaya Mountains; and four days later they arrived at the golden gates of King Janaka's palace.

The king came out to meet the honored sage and offered him and his disciples the welcoming drink of water-sweetened-with-honey. And as they drank of it, the king asked:

"Pray tell me, O Sage, who are your youthful companions, armed with sacred weapons and in their bearing resembling young lions?"

"They are the sons of Dasaratha, monarch of the Children of the Sun, and traveled from their distant home to slay the demons who disturbed my holy rites. It was my wish that they come with me to take part in the contest."

"Welcome, Princes of the Kosalas!" said the king.

And he invited the youths to remain in the palace as his guests.

For twelve days all the customary rites were performed, and the customary sacrifices were made upon the altar. And during all this time a steady stream of guests from every land flowed into the kingdom of Mithila.

On the morning of the thirteenth day, the flood of visitors swept into the vast arena where the contest was to be held. On the side facing the sun were great throngs of spectators who had assembled at the first streaks of dawn. And on the side opposite, the spacious booths, reserved for royal guests from distant lands and adorned with the insignia of the lands from which they came, began to fill with princes and their envoys, preceded and followed by groups of musicians and bearers of the royal banners.

On a platform, far south, the contestants took their assigned places, each wearing the most resplendent costume of his realm. Some wore turbans rich in color; some wore gems whose bright flashes in the sunlight stabbed the eye; and some wore robes of woven gold. Rama and Lakshman appeared in their hunter's garb and deerskin gloves. Yet in their simplicity the royal brothers were more distinguished than the others in their regal robes.

So vast was the spectacle that the eye could not encompass it from end to end.

When all the visitors and contestants were in their places, a blast of trumpets announced King Janaka and his daughter. The great throng rose as they appeared within the booth shaded by the royal canopy, the eyes of all the young men upon Princess Sita, more beautiful than a nymph from heaven.

King Janaka raised his scepter. A hush fell upon the vast multitude.

"At my daughter's birth I made a vow," the king announced, "that her hand would be given only to the youth who had proved his skill with the bow of the ancient kings of Mithila. To the one who shows himself master of the royal bow, my daughter, Sita, shall be given in marriage."

At a signal from the king, an eight-wheeled chariot, bearing the giant bow of the kings of Mithila, was slowly propelled into the arena by five hundred mighty men. All eyes turned upon it as the great chariot was brought to rest before the royal enclosure.

Again the king raised his hand; and the contestants were asked to come forward in their assigned order.

In complete silence the vast assembly waited.

They watched and waited breathlessly to see who would try the seemingly impossible task of lifting the enormous bow.

One by one the warrior princes of many regions strove to budge the bow from its place upon the chariot. They each approached with a flicker of hope, but they all left it with heads drooped in disappointment. Suitors from all the Seven Islands of the Earth tried; and they all failed.

Finally the last of the contestants, Prince Rama, came forward. Thousands of eyes turned upon him as he walked across the width of the arena to the ornate chariot; and the old sage, Vishvamitra, called out:

"Luck be with you, O Prince!"

Rama slowly placed his hand upon the bow, firmly lifted it, and then held it aloft. A great shout rose to the sky. And when the rolling roar of pleasure and surprise died down, Rama began to pull upon the stubborn string. Under his steady arm the string and bow slowly yielded. Closer and closer came the ends of the mighty bow. Then, when the two ends almost met, the bow snapped with a deafening roar.

A cry of exultation went up from every throat, and the prolonged shouts of triumph resounded from side to side of the arena.

At last King Janaka raised his hand to still the tumult, and he announced:

"The victor has won my daughter as his wife!"

Then the king turned to Vishvamitra, saying: "With your consent, O Honored Sage, I shall send messengers to King Dasaratha to invite him and his retinue for the wedding feast!"

The Wedding of Rama and Sita

After the aged king of the Kosalas reached Mithila and had rested from the tiring journey, as father of the groom he signaled the beginning of the marriage rituals with a sacrifice to the gods. And King Janaka, as father of the bride, related to the guests in every detail the succession to his throne (beginning with King Nimi in times long past) to show the noble ancestry of the princess.

At the end of his recital, Janaka addressed Dasaratha: "O King of Ayodhya! With all my heart I offer my beloved daughter to your son. The stars in the heavens are auspicious for a wedding on the morrow. Illustrious Monarch! Begin the day with gifts to the poor — the dowry from each royal spouse to the heavenly spirits."

The following day as King Dasaratha distributed

17

gifts, a young man was brought before him, as envoy from the King of Kekayas.

The envoy bowed low and said: "I hastened here to bring you my lord's message: Our king, the father of your consort, Queen Kaikeyi, is growing old and longs for the sight of his grandson, Prince Bharat. He begs that you send your son to the royal court."

"Welcome," said the king, "and welcome to the wedding feast that soon begins. I understand the yearning of your lord for his beloved grandson, Bharat; and when the wedding ceremonies are completed, he shall go to bring comfort to his grandfather. And I shall send my son Satrughna with him."

Then the king went on with the traditional distribution of gifts to the poor.

On the last day of the marriage rituals, King Janaka and his priests came to Dasaratha's quarters and called out:

"My daughter stands in readiness at the altar, each vow vowed, each prayer prayed, and she as bright and clear as flame! I, King Janaka, her father, now wait for you!"

Dasaratha and his sons followed Janaka into the shrine. There the guests had assembled, and there a sacrificial fire burned upon the altar. As they entered, the altar was sprinkled with perfume by the officiating priests and they brought forward the golden ves-

sels filled with parched corn and rice. Dasaratha led Rama to the altar, to the singing of Vedic hymns, just as Janaka arrived on the other side with Sita.

Then Janaka spoke to Rama: "Here stands my daughter, Sita, ready to assume her duties as your wife. Accept her, O Prince, and take her hand in yours. From this day on, in life and death, she shall be to you as the shadow is to the substance from which it cannot be parted. May happiness dwell with you both!"

As bride and groom joined hands, Janaka sprinkled purified water on them. Three times they walked around Janaka and the sacred fire; next they circled the gathering of sages and priests to the strains of soft music, while they were showered with petals of flowers. Then minstrels started the Wedding Song and the royal dancers began the Wedding Dance.

Still holding Sita tightly by the hand, Rama led her out of the marriage pavilion to their palace chambers, leaving the wedding guests behind at the feast.

At last, and for the first time, they were alone. Rama put his arms around his bride. He looked into her eyes, and she looked longingly into his, as if he were near, and yet very far away.

"No wonder the fame of your beauty has traveled

so far," he said. "Yet I see now that words cannot encompass your loveliness."

"I was doubtful when I first heard of your coming," she confided shyly. "But I was stricken with love when I saw you in the arena, and I prayed and prayed that you would prove your strength with the bow."

"I wish —" Rama began, then fell silent.

"What does my lord wish?" asked Sita, softly.

"I wish that our first hour alone could last forever!"

(And so ends the first book of the Ramayana, known as the Bala-kanda, which means The Youth Section.)

II

The Banishment

(Ayodhya-kanda)

Preparation for a Coronation

ONE DAY the aged King Dasaratha summoned his councilors and said to them: "I have ruled my full measure of years and the time has come for me to announce my successor."

"It is true," they answered, "that you have ruled us well for nine thousand years!"

"It is true," they responded, "that you are sixty thousand years old."

"And it is true," they added, "that from beneath the royal canopy you have blessed our nation, generation after generation."

(This was their way of saying the old king had lived and ruled for a long time. They would say that he had held his breath for a hundred years, to gain merit from the gods; or that he had prayed without ceasing for a thousand years. This was just their way of measuring the monarch's life and deeds with the measure of immeasurable time.)

22

"My sons are each good and worthy," the king continued. "But Rama excels them all. He resembles a compassionate cloud over the parched earth. In valor he is like the gods, and in endurance like a mountain. Envy and wickedness are unknown to him. He loves the wise and honors the aged. Nor can the fool's taunt provoke him to harsh action. He is never rashly swift, or idly slow to fulfill his duty. He listens well; he thinks well; he speaks well. And I wish to see him crowned as Regent of the Realm!"

Those assembled before the king called out: "Ruler of All Men, your decision is most excellent!"

The king looked around in mock surprise, his eyebrows raised, his broad forehead wrinkled, and with a twinkle in his eyes he asked: "How is it you so readily accept my giving up the throne in favor of my son? Have I failed to govern you well?"

"King of our land!" they replied. "We know that in your heart you have long been waiting for a sign to place your first-born son, Rama, upon the throne. The sign is here; and the stars show that the time has come."

The king lifted his hands, palm to palm, and, as if asking for the greatest boon of his life, he said: "Let it be known to my people that Rama will be crowned as Yuva-Raja — raja and king to be!"

Feverish preparations for the coronation began in

the royal capital with great rejoicing. And neighbor vied privately with neighbor to excel in the decorations within and without the home, in honor of the great event.

In the sacred pavilion where the crowning would take place, a hundred golden vessels were filled with unguents, honey, parched rice, and all the other elements needed for the ritual. Lion skins were laid out; bulls with golden horns were stationed in their proper places; and in every corner fragrant incense burned.

As the public gates of the city and arches from street to street were wreathed with flowers and bright banners, royal guests from distant lands began to arrive. And when all the representatives of kingdoms east and west, north and south, had been received by King Dasaratha, a golden chariot was sent to bring Rama before his father.

A solemn hush fell when the chariot drew up bearing the prince. The monarch proudly watched his son alight from the chariot and ascend the steps to the throne with regal grace.

In a voice that could be heard by all assembled, the king proclaimed: "My son, with the consent of the throne, and all our people, it has been decided that you shall be crowned Regent Heir before the moon wanes. You will take your wife, Sita, to the

24

temple and begin the fast you both will keep until you are summoned to the sacred pavilion!"

Rama bowed low to the king, and left.

Prince Rama and Princess Sita went to the Temple of the Kings, and there, alone before the altar, they tended the sacred fire. They prayed silently, then all through the night they watched the sacred flame, withdrawn from worldly thoughts.

And through the night the people of Ayodhya thronged the streets in joyful anticipation of the dawn which would mark the beginning of the ceremonies. In the great squares actors and dancers entertained the crowds with merry plays and songs and dances.

When the hour of blue turned into the hour of gold in the eastern sky and the priests appeared in long processions, the people hurried home to change their linen robes, and in robes of silk hastened toward the route of the royal procession.

Tidings for a Queen

Queen Kaikeyi, mother of Bharat and Dasaratha's favorite queen, was rudely wakened by her old nurse, Manthara.

"Awake! Arise! Unlock your eyes!" Manthara called urgently.

"What evil tidings must I hear?" asked the sleepy queen.

"Peril, swift and sure, is at your door!" Manthara wailed. "I was wakened from my sleep by sounds of merriment beneath my window. And when I went out from the Court of Women, to learn the cause of the festivities, I was told that Prince Rama is to be crowned as Yuva-Raja!" She spoke the words as if they were words of doom.

"But I rejoice in this news," protested the queen as she sat up. "Rama is the oldest of the princes and rightful successor to the throne. He is by all beloved, and I regard him as a son."

"This is not the time for idle dreams and fancied bliss, O simple Queen!" the old nurse scolded her mistress. "Shake off the slumber that still clings about you, and tell me why the king has told you nothing of his plans! Why the haste to crown Rama when Bharat is so far from home! And tell me this: since kings and princes of many lands have been invited to see Prince Rama crowned, why was not your father, King of Kekayas, upon the list of guests?"

Manthara watched distress spread over the queen's face. Triumphant now, the nurse went on to describe with great horror how Rama would soon be lord of all the realm of the Kosalas, and Bharat

would be treated as a mere attendant at the royal court.

As the poison of her words seeped into the queen's mind, Manthara hissed: "When Rama once begins his sway, he will drive Bharat away to distant lands — if indeed, he lets your son remain alive!"

"But what can I do to prevent this coronation?" the weak queen asked in despair.

The nurse came close to her mistress and whispered: "Snatch the crown for your own son! Have Rama banished from the kingdom!"

"How can I do that?" asked the queen, now frightened.

On Manthara's wrinkled face there came a cruel smile. She said: "Do you remember that time the king took you with him when he went to war? And do you remember how you saved his life when he was wounded? He professed to hold you dearer than his life and pressed two boons upon you. You said to him: 'I shall claim them when I need them' — do you remember that?"

"I remember," said the queen, "but that was long ago."

"A king's promise lasts forever," Manthara said. "Now the time has come for you to make your claim."

A King's Promise

When King Dasaratha came to invite his beautiful queen consort, Kaikeyi, to the ceremony of the coronation, she was not in her quarters. He sought her in the magnolia garden with its reflecting pool, and startled the peacocks strutting on the paths as he called her name. Then he came upon Manthara in the garden, and asked for her mistress.

Manthara replied sweetly: "O sire, the queen has entered the Chamber of Wrath!"

Puzzled and exceedingly troubled in mind, the king entered the dark chamber where the queens brought their sorrow. There upon the barren ground lay Queen Kaikeyi, like a branch torn from a tree, or like a young doe wounded by a poisoned arrow.

The king tried to lift her and asked affectionately the cause of her deep grief.

"O tell me," he pleaded, "have you become ill? Has anyone offended you? Speak, and whatever you desire, it will be done — but efface the grief that mars your lovely face and wounds my heart."

"I am not ill, nor has anyone offended me," the queen replied. "But long ago you offered me two boons, and I grieve for fear you will not grant them to me, as you promised."

"Ask," the king pleaded, "and if it is within my power to grant them, they are already granted to you."

" 'The observance of truth is the road to heaven,' " the queen quoted the Ancients. "Swear to me by the thirty-three gods in heaven that you will keep your promise."

"I swear!" said the king. "Now tell me what your wishes are."

"As my first boon," said the queen, her eyes upon her husband's face, "let my son Bharat be proclaimed today your Regent Heir. And as my second boon, banish Rama from your kingdom for fourteen years."

The king's eyes filled with horror. Great anger mounted in his breast, but for a time he could not utter a word. When finally he spoke, his words burned like a consuming flame:

"I married the daughter of a king; yet now I see in her only a venomous serpent! O wicked one, what determined you in this cruelty? Of all my countless followers none has ever breathed a word against Rama. And the throne is rightfully his. Ask any other two boons but these and they shall be yours."

The king looked imploringly at his wife, but her gaze remained fixed upon the ground.

She replied: "A king's promise lasts forever!"

The king pleaded: "I am old and soon must die. Have pity on me. Recall your terrible requests, and I shall give you all that I possess!"

The queen looked coldly at him and with contempt. "You have made a promise, and confirmed it before the gods in heaven!"

The king sank down upon the ground and sat there despairing that words could be found to touch his heartless queen. They remained in silence for some time, the king steeped in overwhelming grief, the queen hardening her heart in determination. Then he spoke to her again, pleading that her request would expose them both to everlasting shame. And when that plea failed, he tried to flatter her, to cajole her into accepting other boons that would bring her greater joy. But his words were in vain, like rain on the ocean's waves. Then, in a sudden burst of anger, the king heaped new reproaches on her head.

Still she stood firm and silent. When at last she spoke, she only said: "Now send for Rama, that you may tell him in my presence of your promise to me."

Celebration into Mourning

The sun had risen high in the sky. The streets were crowded with festive throngs, their eyes shining

bright, their voices ringing out like clear bells in a
deep valley. Flags fluttered in the breeze and the
mingling aromas of sandalwood and incense filled the
air.

In the sacred pavilion all was in readiness: the
priests in their sacrificial garb; the golden vessels; the
seeds and herbs; the royal palanquin with its bearers
standing beside it; and the throne supported by
ivory lions for the Regent Heir.

The shadows shortened, and still the ceremony
did not begin. Wonder began to stir among the people. Their apprehension rose when royal messengers
arrived to summon Rama quickly to his father's side,
and speculations swept through the streets of Ayodhya like a rising wind.

Rama hastened to his father and found him pale,
sitting dejectedly beside Kaikeyi. When Rama approached, bowing to his father and saluting the
queen, Dasaratha's eyes filled with tears. Dismayed,
despairing and distraught, all he could utter was:
"Rama! Rama!"

The prince neared his father and asked: "Why is
my father in such anguish? Have I caused displeasure
in some way?"

"He is not angry with you," Queen Kaikeyi answered arrogantly. "But he has something on his
mind he fears to disclose to you."

Then she quickly reviewed what had transpired.

Prince Rama listened attentively to her words, as if they did not concern him personally and he were a judge in judgment placed. He weighed her words and their content; not how they were spoken, or by whom. And finally he rendered his conclusion:

"A king's promise lasts forever! My father's debt is as my own! Send word to my brother Bharat to return with dispatch to claim the throne which belongs to him by my father's promise. And I shall leave at once, before he returns, so that both my father's promises shall be fulfilled; and none shall ever say that the king, my father, made a promise that he failed to keep."

"Wisely spoken," said the queen, highly pleased her scheme had so well succeeded. "I shall send swift messengers to Bharat. And by your leaving now, you will lessen your father's grief."

Prince Rama bowed his head and walked round his father and the queen three times, palm pressed to palm, paying the homage due them; and then he swiftly left the room.

When it became known to the expectant people that Rama would be banished and Bharat take his place, the festive city plunged into mourning, and the happy chanting turned into lamentation. In huddled clusters, the people exchanged speculations as to what might have caused the strange turn of events.

While the people shared their troubled thoughts and the women of the court wept bitterly, Prince Rama returned to the temple where Sita had remained alone beside the altar.

The princess approached him trembling, her cheeks paling, her lips forming questions she dared not utter. She wanted to ask why he did not wear the coronation robe; why he was not beneath the canopy studded with diamonds like the stars in heaven; why the gold-wrought coronation chariot was not waiting at the door, nor the great elephant which leads the royal procession; why the voices of the priests were suddenly stilled; and why, above all, every sign of joy had been erased from Rama's face.

"I have come to say farewell to you, beloved!" said Rama. And he hastened to tell her of his banishment for fourteen years.

"I shall go with you!" Sita announced without a moment's hesitation.

"O Sita, my beloved, this cannot be! Life in the forest will be full of woe, and you, a princess born, will not be able to endure the black nights sleeping on the ground, the sounds of savage beasts, the roar of thunder under the open sky, the heat of burning days, the thorns that tear the flesh, the bites of scorpions, the hunger when food is scarce, the venomous snakes that by the rivers hide — oh no, my beautiful one, the forest life is not for you! Remain here in my father's palace and wait for me!"

"O Rama! What words are these that you are saying?" Sita put her arms tenderly about him. "I shall go wherever you go, and live however you live. The forest with all its horrors will be like heaven with you beside me; and this palace or any other would be a desolation without you. Say no more. For on our wedding day my father told you that I would henceforth be to you as the shadow is to the substance. Doubt me not, or fear that I shall be a burden to you in your exile. Together we shall look with fearless eyes at mountain peaks when dawn comes; together we shall wade through cool pools covered with wild lilies and watch with delight the white swan and the mallard take to wing. And the root, the leaf, the fruit that you shall get for us to eat, will taste sweeter than nectar. And so a thousand seasons will pass like a single day, if we but spend that day together. Forbid me not, and let me come with you!"

Rama spoke again, and now not of the dangers of life in the wilderness, but of her duty to his sorrowing mother and his grieving father; and of her duty to serve the Regent Heir.

But to all his words she had the same reply: the brother and the daughter, the mother and the son, each had his or her duty. The duty of the wife was to share her husband's fate, for good or for evil. "If you leave me, O Rama, I will surely die! I cannot endure the grief of separation from you for a day; how then shall I endure fourteen long years?"

Rama finally replied: "I would not want to enter even heaven, if that would cause you pain."

"I knew you would not abandon me," said Sita with a sudden smile.

"Come," said Rama, "we must prepare to leave without delay. And before we go all things that we possess should be distributed among those who can use them. For in the years to come our only needs will be a hermit's robe, a staff, and the weapons I shall carry."

As Rama and Sita left the temple for their quarters in the palace, they were overtaken by Lakshman, who had learned of Rama's banishment. He begged his brother to permit him to follow into exile and share Rama's fate. Rama protested that it was his younger brother's duty to remain at home to comfort his mother and their aging father.

Lakshman replied heatedly: "If Bharat fails to care for them as they deserve, I will return and slay him. O noble brother, they have no need of me, but I have need of you. Make me your attendant and companion. With weapons upon my shoulder and a basket to gather your food, I shall precede you wherever you go. Permit me to go with you, my brother, and to follow you into your exile!"

"If you insist on coming, brother, make your farewells to friends and kin, for I shall leave the palace and the city before this day comes to an end."

After distributing their possessions and taking leave of all their friends, Rama, Sita and Lakshman finally went to the White Chamber where King Dasaratha and the queens awaited them.

Dark despair lay heavy on the father's brow when there appeared before him his two sons and Sita, whom he had come to love as if she were his daughter. Tears rolled down the old man's cheeks.

Rama came forward, head bowed and palms together reverently upraised, saying in a clear voice: "Great King, bid us farewell! And bless us with one blessing!"

Every ear was bent to catch the words of the king's faint reply: "Go, my son, my beloved Rama, and return to me safely, before I grow blind, that I may see you once again; before I die, that I may hear your voice again." He paused to keep his voice from breaking, then added: "But oh, stay yet a little while longer — one more day, one more night — that we may prepare a parting feast —"

"I vowed to leave this day, and I must keep my vow as you kept yours, O King," Rama replied resolutely. "Do not waste your heart in longing, nor your eyes in tears, my father. The years will soon pass and we will return to your feet for a welcome, and to your table for a greater feast."

Queen Kaikeyi stepped boldly forward carrying hermits' garments made of bark. "Here is the clothing of your exile," she said. "Put it on now and shed your princely robes."

Rama shed his fine raiment and round his waist tied the hermit's robe. Lakshman followed his example, quickly donning the rough attire. But Sita tried three times to fasten the rough garment, and three times she failed. At last Rama, beside her, hastened to tie the heavy bark mantle over her silken robe, while all the women of the court wept silently.

Now the three were ready to depart. With a last farewell the exiles waited for the chariot ordered by the king to take them to the banks of the Tamasa River which marked the boundary of the Kosala kingdom. And as they waited Rama's mother embraced Sita and blessed her, saying:

"The world is full of beautiful women, so spoiled

through pleasure that they neglect their husbands visited by misfortune. In one short hour the great love proclaimed on the wedding day turns into indifference. But by your action, noble Sita, you shall be forever to all mankind a bright symbol, like a guiding star, of wifely devotion. Care well for my Rama these years in the far wilds. And care well for yourself and Lakshman!"

As Sita made her promise to the queen, the chariot was announced in readiness at the gate. Three times Rama and his companions circled around the king and his queens, bowed their heads in a final farewell, and quickly left the chamber.

When Rama and his wife and brother appeared in the royal chariot in the streets of the city, great throngs surrounded them, crying that they wished to follow into exile.

Prince Rama urged the charioteer to hasten, for drawn-out grief is the bitterest of pain.

"Faster! Faster!" he urged.

Sons, brothers, husbands and wives forgot the bond that joined their lives, forgot their sacred fires on the altars, gave no thought to weariness or hunger, but, like a people united in sudden disaster, sorrowingly followed in the wake of the chariot.

"O charioteer, have pity!" they called. "Draw in the reins that we may gaze a little longer upon our princes and the fair princess. Before, even the rangers of the sky could not look upon her face, yet now she is shown to every passer-by. Have pity! Drive slowly!"

"Urge on your horses!" Rama commanded. "Do not linger. What must be done should be done quickly."

Soon the gates of the city were reached, and the crowds fell behind. The horses galloped faster on the open road, faster than any of the fleetest runners who still tried to keep up with them. Before the evening shadows engulfed the banks of the Tamasa River, the exiles reached it alone, and the charioteer was urged to return to Ayodhya.

Dasaratha's Grief

As Rama and his companions left the court, King Dasaratha rose to his feet, dazed with grief, looking before him with unseeing eyes. Suddenly he broke through the ring of his attendants and ran barefooted from the chamber, calling as he ran: "Rama! Lakshman! Sita! Come back! Come back, my children!"

But they had gone far beyond the reach of his voice. The king hurried through the seventh gate. At a distant bend in the road he saw the dust raised by the chariot. The king called out again in anguish for his children to return.

At last his ministers restrained him, saying: "None may follow too far the departing friend or kin, if he wishes to see him return again."

On being reminded of this precept, the king stopped. He returned to the palace with faltering steps, sank down on a seat of grass upon the polished floor, and hid his face in his hands.

Queen Kaikeyi came to his side and put her hand upon his shoulder, saying: "My master, what is there I can do to lighten your heart?"

Without lifting his head, the king replied in a tired voice: "Touch me not! From this moment I am no longer your master nor you my consort. All that links your life to mine, now and forever I resign and dissolve. If our son, Bharat, takes joy in what you have won for him, I shall forbid him to take part in my funeral rites. Now go, for I do not wish to hear your voice or see your face again!"

Then the king sent for Rama's mother to come to his side.

The gentle queen came to comfort him, and said: "Your eyes shall see him again!"

The king shook his head and replied: "Put your hand in mine, O Queen, for you are now my only consolation!"

They sat in silence like mourners returned from a farewell to the dead. Then words began to come to their lips. They wondered how their children would fare in the wilderness, feeding on roots and wild fruit, resting at night upon the bare ground. Slowly their talk turned away from the painful present to happier speculations of that wondrous day when Rama and his companions would return to Ayodhya; how the people would go out to greet them with welcoming banners and scatter rice over them, and how the songs of thanksgiving would rise to heaven. And in their talk their heavy grief subsided like a receding flood.

When the charioteer, who had carried the exiles to the border of the kingdom, returned to the palace, he was received in the White Chamber of the king.

"O King," the charioteer reported mournfully, "these are the words that Prince Rama said before I left him: 'Go to my father and greet that most illustrious of kings. Tell him that we are well. Say to my mother that it is my wish she should regard my father as if he were a god. Take this message to my brother Bharat, that, though Regent Heir, he should obey his royal father in all things, and to the queens give equal loyalty and homage!' These were Rama's words spoken with bowed head and joined palms."

"And Lakshman, my son, what did he say?"

The charioteer looked down and remained silent for some time before he spoke again. "Prince Lakshman's soul was on fire and he spoke angry words, my king."

"Spare me not, and tell me truly what he said," the king commanded.

"He said: 'For what sin, for what offense was Rama banished? Tell the king that from this day forth my father is Rama, just as he is my brother and my friend. And him alone I recognize as worthy King of the Kosalas.' "

The words fell upon the king's ears like a hail of poisoned weapons on the head of a hunted elephant. When the charioteer ended, the king asked softly, as if fearing the reply: "And Sita, the noble daughter of my friend, Janaka, what did she say?"

"She stood mute between brother and brother, her eyes dim with tears, pleased to hear her husband's words and grieved when Lakshman spoke. But she herself kept silent."

"Tell me again, repeat each detail of all that happened from the moment that you left the palace gate until the moment you returned," the king commanded.

The charioteer repeated his story. And he went on to tell how dreary the groves and gardens seemed on his return; how hushed the birds; how all of nature seemed in mourning. When he entered the city, which he had left so short a time ago, it seemed a different city. The streets were steeped in gloom and desolation. No voice or instrument was heard. Women looked furtively at the returning chariot and turned away with tears and sighs of despair. The city of Ayodhya, from end to end, appeared as unhappy as the queen bereft of her son.

The king listened in silence, but in his heart raged a storm of shame and pain. Long after the charioteer ended his report and left, the aged king sat brooding, drowning in a sea of sorrow and regret, searching his soul for the sin he had committed to deserve such a fate at the end of his long life.

In the days that followed the king did not give up his brooding. And Rama's mother could not break down his barrier of grief. He remained disconsolate, sinking in strength and spirit, until, within a few days, the aged king found rest in death.

In their attempt to bring consolation to the queens, the priests repeated what they always said to a mourner for the dead:

"Such is the Law of the Deed: From good must come good and from evil must come evil. Even at the gates of heaven a soul is ruled by this Law, be it the soul of a beggar or the soul of a king!"

Bharat's Return

Far off in the kingdom of Kekayas, in the city of
Rajagriha, Prince Bharat had grown restive at his
grandfather's court. He appeared one day, dark and
brooding; and when his companions tried to dispel
his sorrow with laughter-provoking tales, the prince
remained as silent and depressed as before.

"We are your friends," they said at last. "Tell us,
why are you so mournful?"

Bharat replied: "I have dreamed a dream that
chills my heart and dims my vision. For I know that
it is full of foreboding."

"Tell us your dream," his companions urged him.

At that moment envoys from Ayodhya were announced to the prince. They soon appeared, still
dusty and travel-worn, and in the name of the Chief
Priest of Dasaratha's court, said:

"O Great Prince, return at once to Ayodhya where
the royal councilors have urgent matters to discuss
with you!"

"O welcome emissaries!" the prince replied. "Tell
me quickly, is my father well? And how are Rama
and Lakshman, my brothers? And the queens?
What message bring you from my father? And what
word from my mother?"

46

The envoys, honor-bound not to mention the king's death and Rama's banishment, answered respectfully: "O Lion among Men, they of whom you ask are well. Fortune smiles upon you, Great Prince, destined for greatness! But hasten, for your return home is impatiently awaited!"

Prince Bharat took leave of his grandfather and traveled eastward with the envoys. Seven nights they camped along the way; Bharat the first to rise each morning, and the last to stop each night, reluctant to allow the weary cavalcade to rest. All through the day he urged them on to go faster, faster, for his heart was heavy with apprehension.

On the morning of the seventh day Bharat's eyes beheld in the distance the great walls of Ayodhya and his spirits rose. But as they neared the city gates, his spirits fell again.

The prince turned to his charioteer, asking: "Why is it that the glorious city, planned by ancient Manu's hand, today stands like a lifeless pile of clay?"

As they entered by the northern gate he asked again, heartsick and dejected: "Why are the streets deserted? Why do we hear no sound of singing? Why does not fragrant incense issue from the doors? How sad and how depressing this Ayodhya I remembered as the Queen of Cities, loveliest in the world!"

The charioteer made no reply, for his lips had

been sealed by the priest's command. Prince Bharat did not understand his silence; but he interpreted it as an evil omen.

As soon as they reached the palace, Bharat hurried to find his mother, Kaikeyi, whom he had not seen for so long. She embraced and kissed him and pressed him to her breast. Then eagerly she asked about her aging father and her kin. Bharat respectfully but hastily answered her questions, pressing upon her questions of his own.

"Where is my father?" he asked. "And how is he? And how are my brothers Rama and Lakshman?"

Kaikeyi revealed that his father had gone where all mortals must be prepared to go in the end. And when her son broke into mourning, the queen told him quickly that Rama and Sita and Lakshman had been banished.

Urged by her son's relentless questioning, the reluctant queen related, bit by bit, all that had happened. Bharat, in terrible anger, reproved his mother, who had expected him to be grateful that she had won the throne for him.

"Though I had no part in this wicked plot," he told her, "yet the stain of it will mark me with infamy wherever I go!"

He left his mother and hurried to Queen Kausalya, and at the feet of Rama's mother poured out his shame and grief, and cursed all those who had brought about the banishment of Rama.

As Queen Kausalya gently tried to quiet him, the priests arrived announcing that the time had come for cremation of the monarch's body, and for Bharat to lead in the rites for the dead.

The prince cried out like a bull whose horns are broken. But the priests cautioned him against excessive grief, and said:

"Three constant pairs each mortal must accept. These are: Loss and gain, pleasure and pain, birth and death. They are all part of human fate."

On the Banks of the Mandikini

When the royal charioteer turned back toward Ayodhya and left them alone, Rama, Sita and Lakshman wandered slowly to the banks of the sacred River Gunga, in the Kingdom of the Hunter, and there they found a boat that took them across to the southern bank. This was their final break and departure. As they stepped ashore and walked into the pathless forest, their long exile began.

With Lakshman walking before and Rama walking behind, Princess Sita was safeguarded between them as they made their way slowly deep into the woods.

"Tonight the daughter of King Janaka will be tested," said Rama to his brother, "with only the ground as her bed, in this forest where no man dwells."

Sita, at a little distance, had stopped to listen to the Indian nightingale, called the Love Singer, as he filled the air with his hymn to the God of the Forests. "How sweet the air!" she whispered. "How fragrant are the flowers! How soft the sounds of forest creatures preparing for the night!"

Lakshman, seeing the ecstasy on Sita's face, said to his brother: "I fear not for the outcome of our Sita's test."

At dawn they rose from their beds beneath the trees, and continued on their way.

They wandered on for many days, hunting, gathering berries and fruit, delighting in the discovery of sights and sounds new to them.

They passed through many forests and crossed many rivers, until they reached a spot, at the foot of the Chitrakuta Mountains where the Mandikini River flows, more beautiful than any they had seen before. The ground was carpeted with flowers and the sweet-scented trees flamed with crimson blossoms and the brilliant plumage of singular birds. And wherever their glance turned they could see majestic peaks of mountains.

They stood in silence and wonder, feasting their eyes and ears and nostrils on the sights and sounds and fragrance about them.

After some time, Rama spoke: "O Daughter of Janaka, O Gentle Brother, here is the spot where we should dwell!"

Lakshman set to work cutting down logs and hewing them into shape. And together the two brothers built a hut and thatched the roof with dry grass and leaves. When their dwelling was completed, they sacrificed a black antelope to the God of the Chitrakuta Mountains. Then they settled down to a peaceful life of prayer, contemplation, hunting, and enjoyment of the wildlife that surrounded them.

The days flowed by; they did not know how many, nor why they should count them. They forgot the court life they had left behind, and no longer thought of themselves as exiles.

Rama and Sita, their eyes beautiful as the lotus, their faces glowing like the moon, would waken with the dawn and roam near the Mandikini River to watch the swans, or cranes and other birds. They swam together in the swift sparkling river, Sita pelting her husband with red and white blossoms and laughingly splashing him with water. When they tired of swimming, they rested on the soft sand of the shore, their eyes upon the distant peaks of the mountains. If Sita said she was hungry, Rama would jump up and in a trice return with pipal figs, or mangoes, or bilwa-oranges, or wild cherries and honey in the comb. As they ate, he never tired of telling her how much he loved her, and his words were sweeter to her ear than the honey to her palate.

Sometimes the three of them would climb the mountains toward a waterfall, white as the royal umbrella, which cascaded down a shaded spot. Or from some lofty height they would observe the rugged mountain shapes in many colors and the purple valleys far below where winding brooks gleamed in the distance.

Rama would say: "I feel no longing for the palace. With you, my love, beside me, and brother Lakshman with us, how can I feel sorrow or regret in this place so like paradise?"

Meeting at the Hermitage

One day, as they stood upon the crest of a high hill, Lakshman suddenly heard a distant rumble. Then his sharp eyes perceived a small cloud of dust rising far below in the valley. They faced the valley in silence as the distant sound swelled, as the cloud of dust grew and rose high into the air. Then they could see quite clearly a mighty army of elephants and chariots and men on foot sweeping through the valley like an irresistible flood.

"Quick, brother!" cried Lakshman. "Take Sita to that cave nearby, and bring your weapons!"

"Let us first see who leads that warlike band," said Rama.

After a long and straining hour of watching, Lakshman recognized the army's leader, and he burst out fiercely: "It is Bharat! He has come to slay us, that his rule may never be opposed! Come, brother, bring your weapons. We shall slay him with our deadly arrows!"

"No, Lakshman! I shall not slay my brother," replied Rama. "I have undertaken to fulfill my father's vow, and I shall not slay my brother. For my loss would be greater than my gain, and men would rightfully despise me. I cannot believe that Bharat has come as our enemy. Besides, he is king now, and we must accord to him the honor due him."

Lakshman curbed his anger and bowed his head.

The three descended from the hill and returned to their dwelling. They kindled a fire upon the altar; then, seated on mats of grass, in silence, motionless, they waited.

At last Prince Bharat appeared within the doorway. When he saw the three hermits, clad in robes of bark, seated upon the ground, his eyes flooded with sudden tears and he fell at Rama's feet.

Rama took his brother's hands, embraced him tenderly and asked: "Is my father well? Is all well with our mothers?"

Bharat sorrowfully told them of the king's death, then related all that had transpired from the time he returned to Ayodhya to the time he arrived at Rama's hermitage. He spoke of his anguish when he learned that Rama had been banished, and the reasons for his exile; and of his refusal to take the place that he felt belonged to his older brother. Then he told Rama of his resolve to find him in the Dandaka forest, to urge him to return and assume his rightful place upon the throne of the Kosalas, while he, Bharat, would remain as hermit to serve out the fourteen years.

Rama shook his head and answered: "A father's mandate may not be disowned by a son. I cannot break the promise I have given to our father."

Bharat bowed low at his brother's feet and argued long and well. He said the throne belonged to Rama because he was the oldest son; and that he was better endowed than any prince on earth to rule the people well.

"O Lion among Men!" Rama addressed his

brother as one addresses a monarch. "Grieve no more for our father's death nor blame yourself. The day once past does not return. The water of the river that flows into the sea never flows back again. Death is forever by our side. It does not leave us when we travel afar — and when we return home it is still beside us. Therefore grieve no more with useless tears for the dead whom tears cannot bring back. Our father has decreed that you shall rule in Ayodhya. Obey him well. And I shall obey him by remaining in exile as I vowed I would."

At last a twice-born priest, who had followed Bharat into the dwelling, took up the Regent's plea: "O Rama, Prince of Princes, Chief of Men! Your father is dead now, and the dead should have no claims upon the living. Come then, and listen to your brother Bharat. Take over the rule that is justly yours and that all your subjects desire."

Rama replied slowly, each word in thought distilled: "Were I to follow your advice, where on that path would I stop in my abandonment of truth and duty? I hold truth to be the cornerstone and foundation of the world. Men justly fear the liar as they fear the venomous snake. And a vow made, whether to one now living or now dead, cannot be disowned without disowning truth itself, upon which justice rests. I took an oath before my father and I shall devote myself to its fulfillment!"

At last Bharat spoke again, in resignation: "Put on these golden sandals of the king, my brother. These I shall take back with me and place upon the throne. And to these sandals shall be delegated all affairs of state. On that blessed day when you return, O Lion among Men, you shall put the sandals on, and, under the snow-white umbrella, take your rightful throne."

Rama once again embraced his brother. Then Bharat and his large retinue started on their long way home.

The Gift of Love

When the last rumbling sounds of the departing warriors had died in the distance, a heavy pall fell on Rama and his companions. The beautiful grounds about their peaceful retreat had been trampled by the feet of elephants and horses. An omen of peril hung in the air; and sadness found an entrance in their hearts.

"We must depart from here," Rama decided. "We shall go on and find a spot that will give us the joy we had, and can no more find here."

Sita and Lakshman were pleased with his decision. They, too, wished to escape from the gloom that had fallen on their dwelling place.

They left the hut beside the Mandikini River and wandered eastward.

In the deep heart of the forest one day they came upon the humble dwelling of an old woman, whose feeble hands trembled like palm fronds in a breeze. Her name was Anasuya, and her fame known to all sages, who called her "Honored Mother," and told of the many miracles she could perform because of her great saintliness.

Sita approached the frail old woman with reverently bowed head and offered to serve her while Rama and Lakshman were away for a short while. The aged Anasuya was greatly pleased with the young princess, and wondered how she came to that deserted spot. While Sita waited upon the gentle old woman, she related how she came to be there.

Anasuya praised Janaka's daughter for renouncing palace life to follow Rama, but Sita replied:

"The praise is not merited by me but by Rama, whose qualities are such that austerities of the wilderness beside him are more pleasing than the banqueting tables of a king."

Sita talked rapturously on and on about the sweet virtues of her beloved prince. A smile flickered on Anasuya's wrinkled face. She took Sita in her arms and urged her to tell how she first met this prince, how he had won her hand, and all that had happened since. And Sita gladly told her.

At last the saintly woman said: "I have been granted the power to bestow a blessing and a boon, and I wish to bestow them on you, fair princess. Tell me your wish, and I shall give it to you and bless you with it."

Sita looked off at the distant hills showing through the branches of the trees, but made no reply. And when the old woman repeated her offer, Sita said:

"What gift is there for me to ask, I who have Rama? Yet, perhaps there is one. On our wedding day my lord wished to stay the hour of our bliss. For his sake, I should like to remain as he saw me on that day."

"You shall have your wish," said Anasuya.

She anointed Sita with a sacred oil and placed precious ornaments and garlands of flowers round her neck. Then Anasuya kissed Sita's forehead, and blessed her, and sent her to Rama.

Rama and Lakshman looked at Sita in astonishment when she approached, garland-adorned, with ornaments about her neck, and more radiant than on the day they first saw her in Mithila during the great contest.

When they were alone, Rama said to her: "Beloved, each day I learn anew how beautiful you are!"

(And so ends the second book of the Ramayana, known as the Ayodhya-kanda, which means The Ayodhya Section.)

III

The Abduction of Sita

(Arnya-kanda)

Years of Bliss

FROM THE lonely spot where Anasuya dwelt, Rama
and Lakshman, with Sita between them, wandered
on from place to place. Often they came upon a hermitage, where coats of bark hung round the humble
dwelling and the ground was strewn with holy grass.
The hermits welcomed the wayfarers with joyful
Vedic hymns, and escorted them on their way with
blessings.

Season after season the three exiles drifted ever
southward, from the northern mountains toward the
southern seas. In the springtime they watched the
birds migrating north; and through the golden autumn days they saw the birds return to their southern homes. During all these periods, night after night
Rama and Lakshman kept the vigil as they changed
watch to guard the slumbering Sita from tigers or
fierce panthers who leaped out of the dark with
burning eyes, intent on killing.

Once a wild boar raced with lowered head toward Sita returning from the river. Lakshman, ever watchful, sent a weapon through the air so forcefully that it began to blaze on its speedy flight to the forehead of the animal. And once a crazed eagle swooped down at Sita's eyes, but Rama's unerring arrow pierced the eagle's heart and dropped him dead at Sita's feet.

These encounters were few; the joyful adventures were many.

They delighted in the sight of trees and flowers new to them. The song of the nightingale at eventide seemed ever freshly sweet, as if they heard it for the first time. They rejoiced in the streams covered with lotus, white and blue and brilliant red; and in the gold and black bees that always sang their busy song near the sacred blooms. Often they saw the meeker creatures of the woods appear across their paths like meadow nymphs; and sometimes they looked eye to eye at deer and doe along the shadow-flecked streams of the forest.

They learned by smell the roots to eat, and the fruits from which to turn aside. And by the very air they breathed they knew when rain would come, or heavy storms, or gladsome days of sunny weather.

Each day brought something new to learn, and they took pleasure in each new thing. The day was long, and yet the season short. The years flowed past. And sometimes it seemed to them that they had always lived beneath the trees beside refreshing streams. Yet there were times too when they spoke of Ayodhya, and one of them would say:

"It seems but yesterday since we left home!"

Tales of the Demons

Wherever Rama and his companions went, they heard tales of the demon giants which lived in the woods about them. These demons (called *rakshasas*) disrupted the sacred rite of sacrifice and often carried off the holy men who performed the rite.

One day, on entering a dark and awesome part of the Dandaka forest, the royal exiles suddenly came face to face with a hideous monster, looming above them like a mountain. He wore a tiger's skin reeking with gore, and on a mighty spear over his shoulder carried three lions, four tigers, two wolves, ten deer, and an elephant head, its great tusks stained red with blood.

At the sight of the three wanderers, the giant issued a roar that echoed in the distant hills.

"How dare you enter my domain? I am the Rakshasa Viradha who slays all saints that come my way. But you are not saints. And how come you to travel with a lovely damsel? Her beauty pleases me, and I shall take her to be my wife."

He reached out to grasp the frightened princess, but Lakshman, swift as a flash of lightning, charged at the monster and toppled him to the ground. At the same moment Rama sped two arrows from his bow, which split the monster's spear at the instant it fell with him.

Sita looked on in horror at the fierce struggle that followed. The brothers struck at the mighty foe with their weapons and their feet and fists, and in the end the giant lay dead before them. They dug a tremendous pit and in it they buried the huge body.

Rama embraced and comforted Sita, saying: "We will hasten away from these wild woods and seek the settlement of holy hermits where peace and goodness dwell."

As they went on their journey, Sita said in her soft voice: "My heart knows how true you are. And yet my spirit is troubled with a fear. I beg of you, lay aside your weapons while we pass through the Dandaka Woods!"

"What harm can there be in our weapons?" asked Lakshman.

Sita bent low her lovely head and said gently: "I remember a story told to me long ago about a holy man. He had in some way displeased Indra, King of Gods, who decided to destroy him. One day Indra came to the hermit in the guise of a warrior girded with a mighty sword, and said: 'O Great Saint, I wish to leave my sword with you until I return. Guard it well and do not leave it out of your sight.' The hermit took the weapon and kept it always by his side. Even when he went in search of roots and fruit he carried the mighty blade with him. As time went on the hermit began to feel secure in the power of the sword, and was tempted to test its strength even on creatures that did not molest him. And so, living *with* the sword, he began to live *by* it. And the sword led to the hermit's downfall, just as Indra had hoped."

"Sweet love," said Rama, "your words reflect the goodness of your heart. I will remember them, and our weapons shall be used only to protect, or to save those threatened with oppression."

The three went on, until their wandering feet brought them to the Forest of Panchavati.

Here they looked about them in silent wonder at the ground covered with scented shrubs and sacred grass, the cool stream flowing through banks of flowers, the bright-winged birds fluttering through the mangoes, the pleasant groves of date palms, and the glistening shimmer of a distant lake.

Rama called out joyously: "Behold! We have reached our home!"

Lakshman gladly responded: "Select the spot and I shall build our dwelling!"

And Sita's fawn eyes shone with happiness.

Lakshman gathered the materials, cleared the ground, smoothed the earth, and under his skilled hands there soon rose a spacious cottage with walls of hardened earth and pillars of bamboo that held up the thatched roof of reeds and leaves and holy grass.

Then the brothers built an altar and offered a sacrifice upon it to the gods of the forest.

And the royal three lived in their cottage in the forest as happily as the gods on high live in their mansions in the sky.

A Woman Scorned

One day at noon, at the time of year when the days grow short and the Himalaya Mountains are ruled by the Lord of Snow, and when the streams of the Panchavati Forest are so chill that even the fowl stand doubtful on the bank before they dip into the icy waters — on such a day, when the sun's rays at noon were no warmer than at sunrise in spring, Prince Rama stood alone waist-deep in the Godavari

River, stately and tall, his voice raised in joyful song.

The prince suddenly became aware that he was being watched. His glance darted swiftly toward the bank of the river like a doe that has just heard a warning of danger carried on the breeze. And there, under a tree, he saw a beautiful young woman who was watching him intently. Rama left the river and covered himself with his hermit's cloak.

The girl approached him boldly, as one to whom nothing has ever been denied, and asked in a vibrant voice: "Who are you in hermit's garb, yet clearly a warrior prince? Why have you come to this wild haunt of giants? And what do you seek to gain?"

Rama spoke to her as one speaks to a child, and told her who he was and why he was there. Then he put to her the same questions.

"I am Princess Surpanakha, from the Isle of the Lions beyond the sea," she replied. "I came across the waters to roam in these forests with my brothers, the giants Khara and Dushan, both brave and fearless bowmen. Our brother Ravan, King of Lanka, is known from sea to sea! Wherever my fancy leads, I roam; and whatever I desire, none can deny me!"

"And what are you out to gain?" asked Rama.

"You!" she answered unabashed. "O best of men, I see my chosen lord in you! Come with me. Let my

fond eyes rest on you and yours on me, and I shall teach you many enchantments."

With a smile, Rama replied: "I have a wife, and you would not be content to take a second place in your wedded life. Your youthful charms may please my valiant brother Lakshman. He has no spouse and you would have no rival in his heart."

Surpanakha turned swiftly to find Lakshman at the nearby hermitage. Without hesitation she boldly told him of her wish to be his bride.

Lakshman, as skilled in words as he was in crafts, replied slyly: "Supremely charming and superbly beautiful princess! One so highborn as you would not be content as the slave-wife of a slave! I am my brother's bondsman, bound by a vow to serve him and his wife, Sita. It would be far better for you to become my brother's second bride. Then he would turn to you instead of his present wife. For who could be so blind as not to see your charms, O loveliest of all female kind!"

The willful and love-stricken Surpanakha turned again to find Rama. And when she saw him in a leafy bower with Sita by his side, her eyes blazed with jealousy, and she rushed menacingly upon the gentle princess.

Lakshman had followed her, and his jesting turned to wrath when he saw Sita's danger. He drew his sword and, before he could be stopped, slashed at the nose and ears of the wayward stranger.

Wild shrieks of pain filled the air as Surpanakha fled into the trackless forest; and long after she had disappeared from view, they could still hear her ominous wailing.

The three looked at each other in deep distress as they listened to the cries of pain recede farther and farther.

Khara's Defeat

Like a thundercloud before the rain, Surpanakha's shrieks reached her brothers Khara and Dushan, surrounded by their men. Then the princess appeared and fell sobbing upon the ground. When she lifted her head and Khara saw his sister's mutilated face, he shouted in fury:

"He who dared maim and mar you shall be served with poisoned shafts, and I vow the birds of prey shall feed upon his flesh before the day is over!"

Khara chose twice seven of his men and told them to slay the princes in coats of bark, nor spare the woman with them. The giants girded themselves for easy victory — fourteen against three hermits, and one of them a woman. They marched off gaily, followed by Surpanakha who seethed for vengeance and longed to witness the massacre of the brothers, and the woman whom they prized so highly.

As they came in sight of the hermitage Rama appeared at the door and warned them not to come any nearer. The giants marched steadily toward him. Rama drew fourteen shafts and placed them all upon his mighty bow. Each shaft, with the swiftness of lightning, pierced a giant through the heart, and all fourteen fell dead. Then there was not a sound, until the princess found her voice and cried out in terror.

Again she fled to Khara and told him through her tears of fright how all the giant crew had been slain by one man with one draw of a mighty bow.

"Dry your tears, my sister," said Khara. And then he shouted: "These brothers shall lie in the dust this day!"

He ordered his brother Dushan, who led the army, to call from among the host of giants fourteen times a thousand of his best men swiftly to destroy the hermits and their hermitage.

"Make ready, too, my chariot," he ordered, "my swords and lances long and keen. On to the destruction of our wicked foemen!"

Dushan mustered the giants, each bearing spear and mace and ax; steel quoit and club and scimitar; pike and lance and bludgeon fierce. They raised bright banners and, to the clang of bells and beat of drums, marched to battle, roaring like lions.

As the giant warriors neared the clearing around the cottage in the woods, Rama ordered Lakshman to take Sita to the safety of a nearby cave in the mountain behind them. And after they had left, he put on his coat of mail, gathered his weapons outside the dwelling, raised his mighty bow, and waited.

Nearer and nearer drew the giants, while louder and louder rose their battle cry. The tumult of their tramping feet and the rolling of the thundering drums echoed through the forest. Like the tide of an angry sea the giants swept on to engulf their lone opponent.

They were almost upon him before Rama let the shafts fly with unerring marksmanship. The first rank of the giants fell, and those behind toppled over them in confusion.

In fearful rage the giant legion advanced over the bodies of their dead, with drawn sword and raised club, with mace and pike, with spear and ax. Their weapons sped through the air like a downpour of steel. Some fell short of their goal and others passed it. Some glanced off Rama's armor like hail upon a fortress. But others reached their mark and dyed his limbs with blood. Undaunted, Rama broke many a well-aimed shaft and murderous blow as he sent his shafts in scores, each gilded arrow glinting through the air for one brief instant before it tore its way through the heart or head of a giant.

Dushan raced back and forth among his men to cheer them on; to rally those who had lost heart; to threaten and cajole his forces whose steady losses mounted as the afternoon shadows lengthened. In frenzied rage he finally rushed ahead and raised his mighty mace, its heavy mass of jagged steel bound with plates of gold. But as Dushan came rushing on, two of Rama's arrows struck the giant's arms from his great shoulders, and the huge body crashed to the ground.

Khara, following behind Dushan, was stung with fury at the defeat of so many of his men and racked with grief at the loss of his brother. He took over the command, and ordered a torrent of weapons poured on Rama's head. And Rama swayed, bleeding from the wounds of barb and arrow.

Khara skillfully released one shaft after another and with perfect aim sheared the joints of Rama's armor, until his coat of mail fell to the ground. With a shout of glee the remaining warriors assailed Rama's exposed body with a shower of arrows, and moved closer for the victory that now seemed theirs.

Although hard pressed and sorely wounded, Rama stood his ground, and watched every movement made by Khara. And as the giant neared in his chariot from which a golden pennant flew, Rama sent a shaft that downed the waving banner into the dust. The baneful giant sent his answer by four piercing arrows that drew blood from Rama's breast.

Rama's every limb was torn by the rending shafts which Khara sent. Once more the prince let fly in quick succession six arrows which killed the four horses of Khara's chariot and forced the giant to come on foot to meet him in single combat. Khara sprang forward, his eyes two red glowing balls of fury.

As Rama's foe neared, the prince cried out: "O slayer of the hermits of Dandaka forest, now reap the harvest of your crimes!"

Khara responded by flinging his mighty mace. Rama broke its flight with arrows which cleaved the monstrous weapon and dropped it harmless to the ground, like a great snake that has been crushed.

Fiercely the giant sprang toward him. Watchful Rama stepped back and sent an arrow that found its resting place in Khara's heart.

There was a sudden stillness in the air.

Lakshman and Sita came out from their retreat, deeply troubled by the sudden silence. Then their hearts lightened. For they saw Rama setting down his bow and turning to meet them.

Sita flew to her husband and put her arms around his bloodstained shoulders. She wept with sorrow for his many wounds, and shed tears of happiness for his great victory.

King Ravan's Plan

While Rama and his companions rejoiced, one giant of the vanquished host escaped unscathed and fled to Lanka, the great city where his king, Ravan, dwelt.

In the royal palace, the Giant King of the Giant Race sat upon his golden throne and listened in flaming anger to the story told by the survivor of the battle with Rama.

The giant monarch, lofty as a mountain, wore regal raiment that sparkled with the lights of precious gems, but his great chest and shoulders were bare exposing the battle scars from sword and spear and arrow. He sat upon the throne of state, a titan and a terror to all those who opposed his will. About him stood his lords and councilors, while at his side hopped a dwarf dressed in bright feathers, darting about like a harefooted ptarmigan, while the king's great golden goblet was filled and refilled with the strong drink made of almonds, sugar cane and persimmon.

The king and his lords listened in disbelief to the

tale of a young hermit vanquishing an army of giants. Prodded by the king, the survivor described the battle and Rama's skill. Though still shaken by the bitterness of defeat, he could not help showing his grudging admiration of young Rama.

"If I had a sword," cried the jester, swooshing his feathery tail, "I would trail this Rama to the river and slice his head off."

"There may be a way in which to destroy this man," said the warrior. "He has a wife who is beautiful beyond all women. Her waist is daintier; her face lovelier; her skin softer; her limbs fairer proportioned than any nymph or dweller of the stars. And Rama so loves her that if she were taken from him, his grief would be more than he could endure."

The mighty Ravan rose up from his throne and roared: "Have my chariot ready! For I shall take from him this fair woman and avenge the death of Khara and his men!"

But the councilors pressed round the king and prayed him to stay his order. They argued that if one man could win against an army of twice seven thousand giants, then his wife, too, might be so favored by the gods that her abduction would bring only destruction to the king, his land and subjects.

"When you come upon the sleeping lion in his lair," they said, "be wise and let him sleep."

Just then his sister Surpanakha entered. Holding high before the king her mutilated face, the princess told her tale of love beside the flowing river, of jealousy beside the leafy bower, and of death and terror on the clearing round the brothers' hermitage.

"It is left for you to avenge our brothers and my unhappy self."

The blood in King Ravan's veins turned into venom as he looked upon his sister's mutilated face. He turned his back upon the royal councilors and roared for his magic chariot to be brought at once. And when the gleaming golden car appeared at the royal gate, the Titan King entered it and flew into the air with the swiftness of a swallow and the roar of thunder on a summer's night. King and chariot soon disappeared from view.

The king did not fly directly to the hermitage in the Panchavati forest. On the way he stopped in the wood of a heart-enchanting shore where his faithful servant, Maricha, dwelt in the guise of a hermit. Maricha had the power to speak in many voices and could change his form at will into that of any living creature.

"Hear me," said the king to him, "and help me attain vengeance."

When Maricha heard the king's plan in which he

was to aid, his face grew white and his eyes filled
with terror.

"O great King, listen to my appeal!" Maricha
pleaded. "Men unrestrained and led by passion bring
ruin on themselves, their people and their country."

But Ravan scorned his words of warning.

Maricha sighed and said: "If this must be, then let
it be now. Come, we will go!"

When they came to the clearing near Rama's
dwelling, Maricha changed himself into a deer, unlike any deer that ever roamed the forest. His glossy
skin was golden, and his narrow face was black with
delicate white markings. His hoofs were carved of
lazulite, and a gleaming sapphire tipped each horn.
He proudly raised his arching neck and raced toward the hermitage, leaping over bushes and disap-
pearing among the shadows of the trees, coming ever
nearer the secluded dwelling, until he was certain
Sita had glimpsed the gold and silver of his skin.
Then he wandered nearer, always keeping within
sight of Sita's wondering eyes.

The Chase of the Golden Deer

"Come! Come quickly! O, quickly come, my lord!
And you, Lakshman, hasten, too!" Sita softly urged
her husband and his brother. "I see a deer, the like

of which has never been looked upon by human eyes. How fair he is, and gentle! O, if only you could catch this wondrous creature, that we might keep him with us as companion!"

The brothers came swiftly to her side and both saw across the clearing the golden dappled deer.

But Lakshman said thoughtfully: "There never was a deer like this! Stay, do not seek to follow him. It is the wicked art of magic!"

Sita, caught in the delight of the enchanting creature, turned away from Lakshman and begged her husband: "O, bring me this fair deer. Its loveliness has charmed my heart!"

Rama was eager to please Sita and made ready to capture the creature alive. Before he left, Rama cautioned his worried brother to don weapons and guard the dwelling against any unsuspected danger, nor leave it for a moment until he returned from the hunt.

Girt with sword and quivers, and with a triple-flexed bow in his hand, Rama hurried into the woods. His eagle eye and sharpened ear searched the long morning shadows for sight or sound of the matchless deer. Soon he saw his golden prey sauntering slowly in full view. Rama neared softly in the shadows until he was so close to the woodland creature he could almost reach out and touch its golden skin.

The deer suddenly lifted his startled head, looked suspiciously around him and, arrow-swift, darted off and disappeared into the shadows like the bright moon hiding behind a cloud. Rama pursued the deer in the direction he had fled but could find no trace of him. The hunter raced this way and that, following each sound. He saw other deer and other forest creatures. But the game he sought had vanished like water seeping into sand. Rama finally stopped to rest in a shadow, ready to give up the fruitless chase. Suddenly, in a clearing within his arrow's reach, he saw the golden deer move slowly, feeding on the grass.

Rama's hope to capture the creature alive was once more revived. He crept forward cautiously, deciding to wound the deer lightly in a forefoot. The hunter raised his bow and aimed the arrow, holding back for one brief moment to sight his target. But in that brief moment the deer leaped into a thicket and was gone. Rama raced after him.

Further and further into the forest, pursued and pursuer ran.

Finally Rama realized that he would not be able to catch the deer alive, and he determined to end the chase by killing it. He aimed one sure arrow that found its way to the golden creature's heart; and the quivering deer fell, mortally wounded.

Rama ran toward his prey. But consternation filled him as he neared. For at his feet lay no wounded deer but the hermit Maricha, in his cloak of bark.

Although the glaze of death was covering Maricha's eyes, he called out in a voice which resounded through the forest:

"O, Sita! O Lakshman! Help me! My brother, help!"

And the voice of the dying Maricha sounded like Rama's own.

Sita heard this frantic, piercing call for help. She turned to Lakshman in alarm and cried: "O Lakshman! Did you hear your brother's anguished call? Speed to him! O quickly save him!"

Lakshman did not stir. "I promised Rama not to leave you," he reminded her.

"You do not love him! Else your feet would hasten you to Rama's side," cried Sita, distraught by fear for her lord's safety.

"Fear not for him, O most fair one." Lakshman tried to calm her. "Even the mightiest of warriors would not dare engage Rama in battle. Have you not seen him vanquish the giant host? Do not ask me then to break my solemn pledge to him. I vowed that I would safeguard you and not leave until his return from the hunt."

Sita stepped backwards and her bright eyes flashed

as she spoke in scorn: "What treachery is this? Can it be your hope that Rama's widow will become your bride? If anything should happen to my lord, I shall drown myself, or leap from some rocky height to welcome death! O base heart! O disgrace of the Kosalas!"

Lakshman replied sadly: "Your words have pierced my ears like spears and are as flame upon my brain." He looked at the burning tears that flowed down Sita's cheeks, and said: "Though evil omens fill my soul with dread to leave you here alone, I shall fly to Rama. And I pray that I may see him safe again beside you."

Lakshman turned suddenly, grasped his weapons, and fled from the hermitage to the forest.

A heavy stillness seemed to fill the air when Sita was left alone. There was a deep silence all about her. Yet in her heart there was no peace. She blamed herself for the cruel words she had spoken to faithful Lakshman; and she blamed herself even more for sending Rama in pursuit of the golden deer.

The Guest

As Sita stood listening to the ominous silence, a stranger appeared before her at the door. Her trusting fawnlike eyes rested on the roving mendicant, upon his red robe of a holy order, the beggar's cup slung over his shoulder, and the sandals of the wanderer tied on his feet.

She bade him welcome and brought refreshing water for his weary feet. She set her woodland fare before him and kindly pressed him to eat.

The stranger's glance lingered on Sita's lovely face as he ate the food set before him.

"Who are you, sweet lady, graced with the beauty of heaven's own Queen of Love?" the wanderer asked. "How come you to this wild spot where giants roam?"

The saintly disguise of her guest deceived the gentle Sita. Faithfully she fulfilled all the duties of hospitality and answered the questions of her guest, while all the while she looked anxiously about for the sight of Rama returning from the chase with Lakshman by his side. And when she had told him who she was and how she came to live in that lonely spot, she inquired politely of her guest — best of the twice-born race — where he came from, and why he wandered without a companion, unlike other men of his holy order.

The stranger rose up from his seat, and as he straightened out he seemed before her eyes to grow as tall as a lofty cedar. He flung aside the hermit cloak to reveal a crimson robe hemmed with gold and edged with rubies, and upon his great arms brightly shone the jeweled bands that showed his royal rank.

"Behold, I am Ravan, King of Lanka, Lord of the Giant Race! Brother of the King of Gold am I; and feared and famed for my valor in all Three Worlds. O fairest of women! The moment my eyes saw your loveliness, my heart was lost to you. And though there are a thousand royal beauties in my court, I shall never look upon them if you will come with me and be my wife and queen!"

Sita trembled with fright. The giant king seemed to her like the Lord of Death. Yet she replied to him in words of biting scorn:

"You would woo me, the wife of Rama! The wife of the best and noblest of all men! As the bat is to the eagle, as the cat is to the tiger, as the jackal to the lion, so are you beside my Rama!"

"You will forget your husband when you come to my palace and my loving arms," Ravan replied. "Five thousand maidens will wait on you, and they will carry out your every wish. Sweet music will precede and follow you wherever you go. Fairer than paradise will be the gardens we shall roam together. And every earthly joy will be yours, as all the days of your life pass in heavenly bliss!"

Sita's cheeks grew pale; her limbs began to fail; and yet she answered proudly:

"O foolish monarch, with the lawless heart! He who seeks to take me from Rama should be pitied. Only disaster can come to him for such an evil deed!"

Ravan pleaded with her and cajoled her. He praised her and he flattered her. And then he threatened her. But all in vain. At last he approached and caught her in his mighty arms.

Sita called out Rama's name in terror. But Ravan

carried the fainting princess, like a dove in the talons of an eagle, and placed her within the enchanted chariot.

As the magic car rose in the sky and flew southward, thundering through the air, Sita's eyes opened, terror-filled. She cried out bitterly for help, and called for Rama and his brother Lakshman.

Her piercing cries wakened from his slumber an ancient vulture named Jatayus. Down he swooped on Ravan with his beak sharp as a sword. The fearless king laid ten brass-tipped arrows on his bow, drew the string as far as his ear, and let the arrows go. Each shaft tore at the vulture and covered him with blood. But the bird rose in a wide circle and, heedless of his desperate wounds, shot down again out of the sky, snapping in two the bow in Ravan's hands. Before the angry monarch could string another and mightier bow, the wounded giant of the air tore away the silken canopy with its royal emblems, broke the pole of the magic chariot, and forced it to descend and land upon the ground.

A fierce and dreadful battle followed between the monarch and the vulture. With claws and beak and wing the vulture scratched and tore the king, his talons ripping through the flesh until they reached the bone. And Ravan, fighting with his sword, returned two blows for every one received, each of his

86

blows ten times as deadly as those of the vulture. Then, with a mighty thrust, quite suddenly, the giant king pierced through the vulture's heart.

The great bird fell to the ground and lay there like the pale gray ashes of a dying pyre.

Sita grieved to see her champion fall and mournfully dropped her flowery wreath upon him as the magic car again rose in the air.

On their journey through the sky to Lanka, she began to drop her jewels one by one in sparkling token of her passing. She scarcely dared believe they would be found; and yet her heart clung to the hope that some might be discovered by Rama and his brother.

Near Ravan's Island of the Lions, Sita spied five monkeys high upon a hill. In sudden glee she drew off a shimmering scarf; weighted it with her earrings; and sent it on its path to the monkeys, whose tawny eyes followed her in curiosity as she passed over them. Sita's hope grew stronger that these tokens of the way she had gone would bring Rama to her.

The chariot flew beyond sight of the hill where the monkeys sat; beyond all sight of land and far over the white-crested waves of the sea. At last they reached the regal city, Lanka, and alighted in the royal court.

The king summoned a palace guard to keep the captive sheltered from the sight of any man or woman, but cautioned them that every care be given her, a queenly bower in which to dwell, the finest robes and jewels for her use, and warned again that all her wishes were to be obeyed as if they were the wishes of the king himself.

Then Ravan hastened to his chamber. Refreshing drinks were brought to him; his wounds were rubbed with healing ointments; and his garments changed for raiment dazzling in its splendor. And thus refreshed, he hastened back to Sita, filled with thoughts of love.

She rested within a bower of marble pillars upon a thronelike ivory dais, against a wall covered with a tapestry of woven gold. And in the jewellike setting of her chamber, Sita's beauty shone like the soft radiance of the silver moon.

Ravan looked at the mournful droop of her delicate neck, at the crystal tears that trembled in her large grief-filled eyes, and he said softly:

"Fair lady, I came to your hermitage seeking only vengeance. But love struck my heart at the first sight of you, and now its burning flames consume me. Show pity for one willing to give up anything you ask. My island home stretches a hundred leagues within the arms of the sheltering water and is as invincible as the ocean that surrounds it. No kingdom can compare with mine in wealth and power. And all I have I lay humbly at your feet, if you will be my queen!"

Sita brushed away the tears that fell upon her cheek, and answered him with scorn: "You carried off by force a helpless woman. But never shall my name be joined with yours. My husband is far away, yet his mighty hand shall strike you down. Your wicked deed will bring you no triumph, and only folly rings in your words addressed to the wife of Rama!"

Her taunting answer enraged the Lord of Lanka. His gentleness melted in the burning heat of his anger and he said fiercely: "Listen carefully to these words of mine and forget your foolish pride. My will is law! My love has made me plead with you. But if within one year you do not overcome your fear of me and return the love I bear you, you shall die!"

Then he turned and stormed out of her sight.

Rama's Sorrow

The brothers Rama and Lakshman returned homewards late in the afternoon, heavyhearted by the omen of the deceptive golden deer. Long before they neared the dwelling, Rama cupped his hands over his mouth and called eagerly:

"Sita!"

Deep in the forest the echo answered faintly: "*Sita!*"

He called again, louder: "Sita! Where are you, Sita?"

And the echo from the distance came back clearly: "*Sita! Where are you, Sita?*"

The brothers looked at each other in dismay and swiftly ran to the open cottage door. They saw the ashes of the altar fire; the bowl and waterpot; a place set on the table as if in welcome for a guest; and yet the cottage was empty and desolate.

Rama scanned every corner and ran from spot to spot, calling Sita's name.

He hurried to the river where she might have gone for water, and in his grief spoke to the trees he passed.

"O katamba tree, have you seen my Sita who so loved your bloom?

"O bell tree, have you seen my fair one who delighted in your golden fruit?

"Sweet tilia, tell me, where is my darling, she who prized your fragrant flowers above all?"

He spoke to the jasmine, the rose apple, the

mango, and the sal. When woodland creatures crossed his path, he spoke to them too, asking:

"Tell me, tell me, have you seen my beloved?"

The sun set and night fell upon them. Still Rama wandered on. He searched twice and thrice in the same places, talking to the shadows, pleading with the gods, threatening to destroy the Three Worlds if Sita were not returned to him unscathed.

At last he came back to the cottage, his heart bereft of hope.

"Do not yield to despair, my brother," said Lakshman. "There are many caves and dark ravines nearby that Sita loved to roam in and explore. We shall search them all and go from ridge to ridge, from crag to crag until we find her."

Lakshman, girt with weapons, started out with Rama by his side. They sought their lost one in every shadowed spot. They scanned the shores of stream and pool. Their voices called into the caverns. But their cries were answered only by the echo.

In his anguish Rama burst out wildly: "O Lakshman! O my brother! There is still no trace of Sita!"

Again Lakshman calmed him with consoling words; again their search went on. But it went on in vain.

The Long Search

Rama was frantic with the pain of his great loss; and Lakshman, filled with dread, suffered mutely, knowing words could no longer reach his brother. Their hopes had wilted like a torn flower lying in the noonday sun.

Suddenly Rama cried out: "O Lakshman, here! A garland — such as Sita wore around her neck!"

Upon the ground they found a bloodstained vulture, lying dead; and they found arrows nearby like the ones used by the giant host, the broken parts of a golden chariot, silk emblems of a canopy smeared with blood, and one half of a mighty sword.

The brothers burned the vulture in the sacred funeral rite, and left the spot hopeful once more that Sita lived and they would find her.

(And so ends the third book of the Ramayana, known as the Arnya-kanda, which means The Forest Section.)

IV

Alliance With the King
of the Monkeys
(Kishkindha-kanda)

In the Land of the Monkeys

THE BROTHERS, in their never-ending search for
Sita, crossed into the kingdom of the Vanars and
came to the shores of Lake Pampa.

Rama looked about him at the trees along the
shore laden with golden fruit and at the majestic
mountain peaks that rose beyond. To his ear came
the interwoven sounds of birdsong, of humming bees
and of a playful breeze rustling in the treetops. And
every sight and sound reminded him of his loneli-
ness; of his longing for Sita.

"O Lakshman!" Rama brooded. "How can I find
delight in this paradise beside the Pampa without my
love near me? Each sweet sound reminds me of Sita's
voice; each fragrant flower, of Sita's hair; each bird,
of Sita's graceful movements! I cannot much longer
live without her and shall surely die. O brother, I

implore you, return to Bharat in Ayodhya, and leave me with my sorrow!"

Lakshman answered steadfastly: "O best of men, cast aside despair; do not abandon hope!"

And as he went on to console his brother, a little man in beggar's clothes appeared, so it seemed, out of the ground. He loped toward them bent forward in a crouch, so that they could not see his face.

While still some distance from them he called out in a high-pitched voice, respectful and reassuring:

"Greetings, best of young hermits!"

Then, as he neared, he continued: "How did you find your way to this wild spot? Who are you, clothed in hermits' bark, yet in every other aspect warriors and princes of a mighty realm? How broad of chest you are! Your shoulders are the shoulders of young lions! And what strange weapons those are you carry!"

He loped around the princes twice and looked up and down at them admiringly.

He cried out again in wonder: "Each of your gold-tipped arrows is like a fiery snake! And behold those mighty swords, gold-hilted and awe-inspiring! Where did you obtain such weapons? Were they bestowed on you by the gods to guard their realm?"

He poured out question after question in a torrent

of high-pitched curiosity. Yet in his curiosity there appeared a design of probing. Suddenly he stopped. He looked up into their faces and asked:

"Why are you silent? Why do you not answer me?"

"Who are *you?*" Lakshman demanded.

The stranger swiftly cast off his beggar's robe. Before them stood a Vanar, long-armed, hairy all over, with a long tail, his brow wrinkled, and his sad eyes looking upon them kindly and wise. For in outward appearance the Vanars were like monkeys, with tails and claws; some huge as bears and others small as ring-tailed lemurs.

"I am Hanuman," the Vanar told them, "son of the Wind God, chief of the armies of Sugriva, banished ruler of the Vanars! My lord and king saw you from that distant hill. He sent me to learn whether you come in peace or as the envoys of King Bali, his older brother and worst enemy."

"We come in peace, although in sorrow," replied Rama. "The fame of Sugriva the Righteous has reached us and we have yearned to meet him face to face. Now he has graced us through his envoy, whose words flow sweetly with neither pause nor haste."

Lakshman related how they had been banished from Ayodhya and all that had happened to them since their banishment. He described Rama's battle with the giant host and Sita's disappearance soon afterwards. He told the Vanar of the dead vulture they had found and the signs that led them to believe Sita had been abducted by Ravan, monarch of the giants.

"We have other tokens," said Hanuman.

"What tokens are they?" asked Lakshman.

"One day my king and I and three others beside us sat on the top of a high hill. Above us King Ravan flew by in his magic chariot. The king was bloodstained and the canopy above him torn away so that we saw the fair woman with him. As they passed, we heard the woman cry out: 'Rama!' and 'Lakshman!' and then she threw down an amber scarf to us. We picked it up and followed on the ground, keeping Ravan's chariot in sight. And as we followed, we found an anklet and a bracelet that might be hers."

Hope revived again in Rama. "Where are the tokens?" he cried out in haste.

"We have them in our mountain cavern," Hanuman replied. "Come with me to King Sugriva, and he will have the tokens brought to you."

King Sugriva's Story

At the mountain retreat Hanuman presented the brothers to the banished king and told the monarch

97

of their origin and the reason for the princes' presence in his land.

The king welcomed the princes with outstretched hands.

Hanuman hastened to strike a flame by rubbing wood on wood, then quickly lit a fire upon the altar. Before the sacred fire the king and his guests vowed friendship in a bond never to be broken.

"O Prince," said Sugriva after the altar rite with Rama, "like yourself, I am an exile; and like yourself my wife has been torn from my side. I know your sorrow."

Attendants set food before them in the cool shade of a sal tree. And as they ate, the king told the guests his story:

"At my father's death, my elder brother, Bali, was crowned king, and I served him faithfully and well. One day the Giant Mayavi challenged Bali to a fight in single combat for the love of a woman both desired. I cautioned Bali against this, but he agreed to meet the challenger. And, as was my duty, I went with him to be at his side in triumph or defeat. When Mayavi saw Bali coming, he turned away as if in fright and fled into the mouth of a cavern. 'Wait for me here,' my brother commanded, 'while I go in and slay my foe!' I sat down at the entrance and waited. I waited through the day and night; and then I waited till a full year had passed. Still Bali did not come out of the cavern. I decided that my brother had been slain, and sealed the entrance of the cave with a huge rock to keep wild beasts from entering. Then I returned to the palace to report all that had happened. The ministers of the court were certain Bali had lost his life, and they crowned me Regent. And for some time I ruled with my beloved queen beside me.

"Then one day Bali appeared. His eyes were red with rage and his heart hardened with pride. Though I bowed low before him, glad to restore his throne, he only reviled me, and ordered the execution of the councilors who had crowned me. He accused me before the people of conspiring with Mayavi to destroy him. He claimed he had been tricked into the cave and I had barred the way out with a rock so that he could not escape after he had killed the giant. No matter how I proved his accusation false, his anger would not subside. He drove me into exile, and took my wife as his own."

Rama was deeply touched by his host's recital. "For such wrongdoing, your brother Bali deserves to die," he said. "I, who know what grief must fill your heart, shall free your wife with my bow and return the kingdom of the Vanars to you. For though your brother is the elder, his heartless actions prove him unfit to rule."

Sugriva shook his head in despair. "I do not doubt your kindness, but you do not know my brother Bali. He is shaped like a great bull and has the strength of a thousand elephants."

Rama rose from the ground, lifted his mighty bow, placed an arrow upon the string, then let it fly. Like a shaft of burning gold it cleft seven stout palms in a row, pierced the side of a hill, and finally returned to the bowman.

King Sugriva, overwhelmed by this feat, bowed low to Rama, hands pressed palm to palm, and said: "My doubts have vanished! Not even Indra, God of the Clouds, is a match for you! Come, subdue my foe, who bears a brother's name!"

The Fall of Bali

Led by Sugriva and Hanuman, and followed by their men, Rama and Lakshman set out for Kishkindha, the Vanar city.

When they came to the outskirts of Kishkindha they concealed themselves in a dense green forest nearby. Sugriva alone approached the city gate and in a wild sky-piercing cry challenged his brother Bali to meet him in single combat.

His shout was so loud that the bulls in the pastures fled like frightened deer. And the challenge reached Bali's ear like thunder.

Bali rolled his eyes and gnashed his teeth, not believing that Sugriva dared return with such a challenge. The earth trembled under Bali's feet as he rushed out to crush his brother.

With fists like thunderbolts the two rushed at each other. Now one, now the other was downed by a blow. But each time they sprang up again to take and to give blow for blow. Their robes were soon torn in shreds and stained red with blood. Fierce and fiercer grew the combat, and the sound of their mighty blows mingled with the hissing of their wrathful breathing.

Sugriva grew weary and faint from the loss of blood which streamed down his sides. He gathered all his unspent force and tore a tree up by its roots. Using it as a lash, he smote his brother over the head until Bali reeled and sank to the ground. But Bali was not down for long. He rose with a huge rock in his hands and advanced toward his quailing opponent.

At that moment Rama placed an arrow on his bow

and sent it to its goal. It pierced Bali's breast, and the mighty king fell like a toppled oak.

Bali called out to Sugriva for forgiveness as his eyes dimmed behind the mist of death. He said faintly to Sugriva who was bent over him:

"The Vanar realm is yours now. Rule it well. There is one boon I must ask from you before I die. It is not an easy thing for me to ask. Care for my only son, Angad, as if he were your own. And bring him up to be as brave and resolute as yourself."

Sugriva's sweet victory turned bitter when he heard his brother's last request. And when the people came to look upon their slain monarch and weep for their mighty chief, Sugriva mourned with a deep mourning.

At last Rama spoke to the assembled people: "Cease your lament. Grief cannot bring the dead back to the living! The fate that determines each word and deed determined Bali's end. Now is the time to honor him in the sacred funeral rites which are the due of warriors."

After the lengthy rites for the dead king, the Vanar lords surrounded Sugriva reverently and wished to crown him.

Sugriva took the golden chain of royal office from them and placed it about the neck of young Prince Angad, saying: "The throne and realm are his. But until he reaches the age to rule, I shall remain as his regent, and take his place beneath the white umbrella decked with the king's gold."

Sugriva was crowned with all the honors due a king. The sacred waters were poured upon his head. And glad shouts rang out from the people:

"Long live our Regent and King!"

The Season of the Rains

King Sugriva entered the city of Kishkindha with his people, and proclaimed a festivity to celebrate the coronation.

Rama and Lakshman did not enter Kishkindha, bright with banners and gay with the noise of merry-making throngs, for the vow taken by them when they left the royal capital of Ayodhya did not permit them to enter the gates of a city.

Until the season of the rains was over, in that roadless, pathless land nothing could be done to gather the armies or dispatch spies in search of Sita, as King Sugriva had promised. The hermit princes settled in a cave high in the mountains to await the seasonal rains that were almost upon them.

From their lonely retreat the brothers could observe the tiger and the deer. They could watch the lordly lion in his chase. Flowering vines covered the trees about them; and in the treetops monkeys chattered ceaselessly. Their cave was spacious within; and neither rain nor wind could reach them. The entrance was guarded by a sable-hued rock, long ago severed from the parent rock on the mountain far above them. The cave provided them with safe shelter; the trees nearby gave them abundant fruit; and there was all around them dead wood for the altar fire.

Lakshman was enchanted by the green wonders that surrounded them and often exclaimed in his delight. He called Rama's attention to the winding river far down below them; to the little gemlike islands on its bosom, and the sandal trees that fringed its bank. He listened to the shrill voice of the peacock, to the soft notes of the gentle nesting birds, and pointed out to his brother the changing clouds that sometimes took the shape of herds of elephants in wild stampede.

"A lovelier place than this there cannot be!" he cried.

But Rama found no comfort in the pleasant sights about him; and sorrow tinged his every thought.

Again and again they spoke of the hope of finding Sita, and of destroying the fiend that had abducted her. But the long months of waiting were before them, while the rains kept them within the cavern, as if they were imprisoned.

The clouds that rose as white-clad hills were slowly transformed into shadowed mountains of the sky. The darkened air grew still. No bird, no insect could be heard or seen. From east to west the sky was cleft by red lightning flashes that lashed the heavy skies. A sudden wind began to moan along the cavern's mouth.

Then the rain started. At first huge, rare drops fell, each making an individual splash and stain. The lily and the lotus closed like quickly shutting eyes. The slanting drops increased in number, and with sudden fury turned into a downpour. Streams flowed down the rocks like tiny waterfalls.

The downpour slackened. But the rain continued as a shower or drizzle. It went on through the day, and it went on through the night. The cloudy morning revealed a world damp and cold and waters streaming on all sides, corroding the soft earth and carving deep into the sloping sides.

Sometimes there would be a rift in the clouds and the sun appeared; and then the moving clouds would cover it again. And day after day the rain would fall.

Rama grew more restless with the passing of each day in the dry cave. But Lakshman would remind him that each day brought them nearer to the time when they would be able to search once more for Sita.

The Gathering of the Armies

At last an end came to the season of the rains. And King Sugriva called Hanuman to his side, saying:

"The time has come for us to fulfill our pledge to Rama. Gather together all the Vanar legions!"

Hanuman dispatched swift messengers to the east and west, to the north and south. They went over hills, through woods and over lakes. They brought their message into hidden groves and up mountain crags and wherever Vanars lived, to sound the alarm and order the king's legions to gather near Kishkindha.

Three million Vanars from the wooded regions, fierce and strong, answered the king's call. Ten million more, with coats like burnished gold, came from the warm valleys. From the Himalaya and other ranges came still another hundred million Vanars, their manes like those of lions, fearless and eager for battle. From the palm groves and the betel woods, from mountain caves and lake dwellings came countless numbers more, varying in size and color and in fighting skill. But all were eager to take their part and obey the king.

There were white ones among them who lived at the snow line of the mountains; and golden-haired ones that never left the warm groves in the southern valleys. There were indris, aye-ayes, pottos, as well as apes, baboons and chimpanzees.

Though in outward appearance the Vanars seemed like monkeys, in reality they were the off-spring of the sun and moon and wind. They could talk. They could think. They could judge between good and evil. Like the giants, they had extraordinary powers and could assume any form they chose. They could, at will, grow huge as an elephant; and, in the twinkling of an eye, change into a creature the size of a cat or even a mouse. And since they were beings with four hands, as all monkeys are, they could walk with ease among the treetops and leap through the air as if they had wings.

One trait all the Vanars had in common: they prized what was right and warred against evil.

Now they gathered like clouds, some silver-white as the shining moon; some tender green or lotus-blue; some white-coated like virgin snow on the mountains from which they came. On the great plains they assembled in warlike pride, waiting for the king to issue his commands.

A hush fell upon the multitude as the king appeared. He explained the reason they were gathered there, speaking to them as a father would to his assembled sons. Then he entrusted assignment of the varied tasks to Hanuman, chief of his armies, and considered by all the greatest of the brave Vanars.

Hanuman dispatched one chief with his host to search the eastern region. Another he entrusted with the task of scanning the plains of the west. Still another chief was sent with his men to search the north. The south, as far as the shores of the southern seas, Hanuman himself undertook to survey with the warriors he had chosen to serve him.

"Best of Vanars," said the king to Hanuman before he departed, "nothing can stay your rapid way by land and sea! Since you can leap and fly as high as the House of the Immortals, nothing will be hidden from your searching eye. Go, then, and bring back to Rama news of his beloved wife!"

"And if you find her," said Rama, who had listened to the king's words, "give her this ring that bears my name, that she may know you are my envoy whom she may trust."

Hanuman took the ring and bowed.

He issued the command to all his chiefs, and the Vanar legions began to disperse like clouds of locusts flying in all directions. Soon no sign was left in the great plain of all the hosts that had so recently gathered there.

Son of the Wind

Rama and his brother were left alone.

King Sugriva came to their retreat to reassure them. They sat in the pleasant shade of an asoka tree whose immense clusters of golden flowers formed a regal canopy above their heads, and the king told the princes many tales about his land and people.

Rama listened politely, but on his face was a look of dark despair.

"O Rama," said Sugriva, "despair is the serpent's poison and should never enter a noble mind. I know my Hanuman, Son of the Wind, and he will not fail you."

"Why do you call him 'Son of the Wind'?" asked Lakshman.

"There was once a nymph," related the king, "fairer than all the nymphs in heaven, and her name was Anjana. But Anjana did something which displeased the gods and was banished from heaven to live as a Vanar child on earth, though her wonderful beauty and immortal shape were not taken from her. One day the God of Wind saw the incomparable Anjana and fell in love with her. He approached and fanned her silken robe, frankly admiring her charms. Anjana did not know he was a god and became terrified. But he reassured her and said: 'Fear not, Anjana, and trust me. For you shall have a son who will never grow tired and, like his father the Wind, will be able to leap three hundred leagues above the ground.' Anjana rejoiced, and when her son was born she knew he was destined for marvelous deeds. That is why I call Hanuman 'Son of the Wind' and why I know he will not fail us," Sugriva concluded.

"But why do you call him 'Hanuman,' which means Broken Jaw?" asked Lakshman.

"While still a small child," the king replied, "he

leaped up to a great height and his jaw was broken by a bolt of lightning. It was then that he was given the name Hanuman. His father was so incensed at the God of Lightning that he stilled the breath of the world, so that not the softest breeze would blow. And terror filled all living things, for without wind the world cannot long endure. To placate the God of Wind, Hanuman was given the boon that no one should be able to kill him with any weapon made of steel."

The Barrier of Water

As Hanuman and his hosts moved southward they searched every cranny, questioned every traveler and, wherever they could, spied for information that would lead them to Sita and her abductor. Finally they reached the shores of the southern sea.

Hanuman and his troops agreed that if Sita was still alive and kept prisoner by King Ravan on his island fortress, she must first be reached in secrecy and the circumstances of her imprisonment discovered, before they could plan her release. But the city of Lanka on Ravan's isle was separated from the mainland by a wide arm of the sea. How could Sita be reached?

"Let me try," said one powerful Vanar, "for I can leap a distance of ten leagues."

"That is not far enough," said Hanuman.

"Then let me try it," said another, "for I can leap twice that distance."

"A mighty leap," said Hanuman, "but not far enough."

Others came forward who claimed they could leap thirty, forty, fifty, sixty, and as high as eighty leagues. And to each Hanuman gave the same reply:

"Not far enough."

Then one great sage, whose age was equally great, came forward humbly. "There was a time in the prime of my youth when I could leap so far as to circle all the way around Vishnu the Creator. Even now I feel the fire of youth within me burning, and I feel certain that I can leap as far as ninety leagues away, if my poor leap will be of any avail."

"Still more is needed, Great Sage," said Hanuman. "A hundred leagues separate us from Lanka. And I alone can clear that distance."

With one great shout and one great leap Hanuman went up into the air swifter than an eagle. From down below, his men could see him land on the ledge of a very high mountain. There he stood for some time, like a diver on a great height before making a plunge, looking sharply across the wide sea that lay between him and his destination on the Island of the Lions.

(And so ends the fourth book of the Ramayana, known as the Kishkindha-kanda, which means The Kishkindha Section.)

V

The Beautiful Story

(Sundara-kanda)

Ravan's Palace

HANUMAN PRAYED to the Sun, to Indra and to the
God of Wind. Then he mustered his full strength
and sprang from the ledge on the mountain height.
Across the ocean he passed like a ship in full sail before a gale holding its venturous course above the rolling waves. And soon through the boundless fields of
heavenly blue he saw the long dark line of woods on
an island fair and green.

He reached the distant shore and alighted on a
mountain peak and there he gazed down on the shining domes and glowing turrets of the city of Lanka,
glittering like a crown. He looked in wonder at the
glorious city with its lotus pools, its fountains sparkling in the gardens, its groves of trees with blooms of
every hue. On the city walls bright banners waved in
the breeze, and the gold-burnished gates shone dazzling in the sun.

The Vanar waited outside the stoutly fortified city
until nightfall. Then he changed his form into that of

a fox-nosed lemur that in the moonlight seems no bigger than a cat. And in that shape he stole into the city.

Through all the broad and pleasant streets he roamed, past mansions like the soft-hued clouds of autumn skies. From their great latticed windows came soft light, and music, and joyous bursts of laughter, while on the perfumed air the tinkling chime of silver anklets blended with the sound of women singing and the chant of minstrels.

From street to street and court to court the Vanar hastened, searching every face he passed. Among the crowds that thronged the streets sped eager envoys, tonsured priests, and warriors in royal mail who carried maces, bows and flashing swords. These soldiers Hanuman followed in his search for Rama's queen; and they led him to a walled-in palace towering on a mountain crest, surrounded by lotus-covered moats. The glittering gates of the palace were guarded by sentinels, elephant-mounted, and rows of sentries in gilded chariots.

Beyond the palace gates he glimpsed long lines of noble courtiers; and tabor, drum and shell filled the soft evening air with music. Within, unseen, a retinue of women clashed tinkling armlets in their dance, and it came upon the breeze like music of a distant sea.

A stream of guests, minstrels and royal attendants constantly flowed into the royal court; and Hanuman, the lemur, slipped by with them unnoticed. Within the walls, the spacious halls receded in depth like an enchanted forest. Each hall he entered seemed more dazzling than the one before. And silk-robed women passed, their beauty bright as lightning in a darkened sky.

Hanuman roved on his light tread from hall to hall, and through every garden and through every bower for soft delight. He saw feasting tables laden with great delicacies, and royal arms wrought in gold and silver. And then, more marvelous than all the rest, he came upon the monarch's magic chariot.

Hanuman gazed rapturously upon the car. Bright as the sun it stood, with gems inlaid, and each part wrought with lavish care. And in it, as in a car of Paradise, the king could travel through the air with all the splendors of a royal palace. Hanuman walked round the chariot, with every fair device, perfected by the Architect of the Gods.

Then he turned away from the wondrous car and stealthily moved from wing to wing, his eyes searching every woman's face. But nowhere could he find a trace of Sita.

Past midnight Hanuman entered a hall whose regal splendor showed it was the dwelling of the king.

Great jeweled arches shed their gentle luster on golden pillars rising far below. And gem-encrusted stairways rose up from the crystal floor. Upon the air stole the sweet scent of trees hung heavy with their ripening fruit. Through the open doors appeared the silver flash of swans; the wreathing smoke of fragrant aloe; the shine of almandine and chrysolite.

At last the Vanar reached the ladies' bower. There dwelt the princesses the king had won in battle, or by force abducted from their homes.

The revelry was over. The hall with fretted roof and painted walls was quiet. And on soft carpets, overcome by sleep, the graceful women lay like lovely lilies on a silver lake.

One sleeper frowned; and on another's face a faint smile lingered. A queenly woman rested in slumber still as death, her head thrown back, her arm outstretched upon the garland fallen from her brow. Near her lay one curled up in childlike grace, her small feet bare, and bare her arms. One slender girl within her arms clasped tight a golden lute, her sweet head like a lily bent on it. Another sleeper's gentle breath blew softly on the lace that touched her lips.

Hanuman moved quietly among the sleepers, searching every face for Sita. But he searched in vain.

Through an archway opening beyond the women's bower, the envoy of the Vanars saw a regal couch. It stood upon a crystal dais, beneath a canopy as pale and soft as moonbeams. And there, on skins of sheep and deer, lay Ravan in his glittering robes, eyes closed in sleep, the powerful arms extended, their great length covered with jeweled armlets. Hanuman recognized the king, whom he had seen the day Rama's queen was carried through the air.

Hanuman returned to his quest, scanning each face, exploring each corner and searching every part of the palace with eager eyes. Finally a black fear came to him.

He thought: Perhaps I search for one who no longer exists. The beautiful Sita may have jumped from the chariot over the ocean and now lies buried beneath the waves. Or she may have reached this place and died of anguish.

The more he speculated, the deeper grew his despair.

Then he noticed above a high barrier the bright blooms of an asoka grove. He leaped over the wall and swiftly followed the green pathways among the trees. He came upon a lake starred with lilies, whose waters lapped on crystal steps. Hanuman climbed into the branches of a great tree and there he brooded through the night.

In the Asoka Grove

When the sky paled in the East, Hanuman noticed the coral colonnades of a pavilion; and there beside the gently flowing stream a slender woman softly weeping, her face pale as the crescent of the new moon.

"This is she!" Hanuman cried out. "The lotus-eyed! The captive beauty borne through fields of air! This is she, fair as the moon!"

About the weeping lady stood sullen guards, frightful to look upon in their disfigurement. And Hanuman wondered within the leafy shelter of the tree how he might speak to the sad queen alone.

Then, as the light grew strong, he heard the strains of music and the priestly chant of morning hymns. Into the grove danced a hundred silk-clad maidens, their ornaments tinkling music as they came. Some carried gold urns filled with water; some bore precious platters heaped high with rare fruit; and some bore scented wine in gem-encrusted bowls.

Within that retinue of beauty towered the king in a scarlet, gold-embroidered robe. And as they neared the stream where Sita sat, the monarch's eyes shone bright with pride and love. A clash of cymbals overlaid the beat of muted drums as Ravan stopped beside his captive.

She did not stir. Her hands were folded on her breast, like frightened birds; her eyes downcast to turn away from the king's bold glance.

"Give up your grieving and dismiss your fear," said Ravan in a voice soft as black velvet. "O lovely lady, do not hide your beauty from my glance. At your sweet feet my kingdom I will lay. The whole rich world I'll conquer for your sake. O pearl of women, show my great love a small sign of your favor!"

Sita sighed. Then she answered gently: "Be wise, Great King! Do not woo a love that never can be yours. Save Lanka, that it may not perish through your sin. Restrain your lawless heart. For my heart belongs to Rama now, and ever will!"

Fiercely Ravan's anger raged. "Your wayward spirit flaunts a lover's words. And still my love for you restrains my anger, as the bit checks the unruly steed. Yet this must be your last respite. And two months hence you shall choose between my love and death!"

"I shall forever so remain," said Sita, softly.

"I shall not forever so restrain myself," replied the king. He turned angrily away and left the grove, the lovely women following in his wake.

The hideous guards again encircled Sita.

One said wonderingly: "How can it be you do not prize your choice as mighty Ravan's bride?"

Another said: "Come, do not let your folly cast aside the life of happy queen!"

And one among them said: "Scorn not our words, O lady! Seek the king's love, or you will surely die!"

Like a lost fawn the princess trembled among them and her hot tears flowed.

Then one of the jailers whispered to the others: "Last night I dreamed a dream and to this hour my blood is chilled by the remembrance of it. For I saw this lady clad in white beside her husband, Rama. High through the sky they flew in Ravan's chariot, while Ravan, shaven and disgraced, lay stricken in the dust. Then I saw fair Lanka lying in ruins and the waters of the sea rolling through our golden city. Be gentle with the lady now, so that your lives may be spared later!"

The band of jailers looked in fear upon each other. Then, whether in dread of Rama's vengeance, or in the wish to please the lady should she turn to Ravan, one by one they slipped away, knowing their absence would please the prisoner.

Sita crept beneath a bright asoka tree and on the bare earth, wild with grief, she wept:

"O woe, that I may not leave this life I loathe!"

Hanuman Reveals Himself

No wind blew, no breeze stirred, as Sita sorrowed on the ground, and yet the petals of the flowers above her head began to fall like sudden summer showers. Sita's tear-filled eyes turned upward. And there she saw a small fox-nosed monkey with a long, dark tail, whose kindly eyes were fixed pityingly upon her. He sat there swinging the bough and shaking petals down to snare her gaze. When their eyes met the bough quieted, and he said softly:

"I bring you greetings, Daughter of Janaka!"

Sita rose quickly, trembling at the mention of her father's name. "Who are you?" she whispered.

"I am Hanuman, a chieftain of King Sugriva's armies, and his envoy!"

"And who is your king?" she asked.

"He rules the Vanar kingdom and is your husband's friend. All his many legions he has sent in search of you. And now, at last, the long-lost queen of Rama has been found!"

Sita shook her unbelieving head: "Is this a dream?" she asked herself. "And yet a dream it cannot be, for sorrow has not let me sleep. Is this a phantom conjured by distress?"

The monkey nimbly clambered down and stood

before her, small and humble. "I am neither phantom nor illusion, but the envoy of a king," he said.

But Sita had recoiled from him as if in sudden danger. "How could you be a Vanar when many leagues of water lie between your shores and Lanka?"

"O fair of face," said Hanuman, "I am a Vanar." And then he revealed to her that as Son of the Wind God he could leap from shore to shore. "Sweet lady, are you that Sita whom Ravan carried from the Forest of Panchavati?"

"I am that Sita!" she replied.

"Then gaze upon this and tell me whose it is," said Hanuman, extending upon his open palm the ring of Rama, bearing Rama's name.

Sita took the ring she knew so well and happy tears flowed down her cheeks. "O noble envoy, speak! Tell me of Rama! Say, is all well with him? Is loyal Lakshman at his side? When will my lord come and free me from this isle?"

"Your lord is well and longs for you, but knows not where to seek his lady!"

"Brave envoy, go to him!" she begged. "O swiftly go! Tell my dear lord two months of life remain for me. Two moons remain, and if I am not freed, I shall be slain!" Then Sita drew out from her hair a sparkling gem. She put it in the hand of Hanuman,

and said: "Take this token to my lord and it will
bring him the joy his ring brought me. O quickly go
— I hear the guard returning."

The Vanar chief leaped up within the tree, but
before he disappeared from view the jailers caught
a glimpse of him. They turned angrily on Sita, de-
manding the stranger's name, and how he dared to
speak to her without the king's consent.

Hanuman Captured

As Hanuman went on his way he felt an overpower-
ing wish to give Ravan a foretaste of what Rama
and the legions had in store for him.

"Of the four ways to deal with a foe," he thought,
"the first is conciliation — but Ravan will not be
conciliated. The second way is to placate him
through gifts — but where are those gifts that could
suffice to win King Ravan? The third is to sow
dissension among his subjects — but Ravan's people
worship his great strength and will remain loyal.
The fourth way is force; and force alone will touch
the giant king."

The wondrous monkey set out to lay waste the
royal gardens. Tall trees crashed about him and
startled birds escaped from their nests with fright-

ened cries. As Hanuman went on he left a wilderness behind which looked as if a wet monsoon or fire had passed that way.

From out the palace came the royal warriors brandishing battle-ax and sword, burning for battle. And as they sought their foe, one of Sita's guards ran up to them, shouting:

"There! That is he! The one we saw within the grove, who talked to the captive lady! All lies in ruin now save the one tree where Sita sits alone!"

The king in burning fury ordered his men to crush the creature in monkey form. Hanuman did not flee or hide. He leaped into the air as the warriors clustered thick about him, like moths around a flaming torch. Hanuman taunted them and caught the spears and battle-axes that they flung to kill him. He threw them back upon the warriors, slaying the foremost of their leaders. The greater their losses, the greater grew the men's rage and their determination to destroy him. They bombarded him with poisoned shafts. Hanuman leaped into the air beyond the limit of the arrows' flight. Then he roared and fell upon the army, toppling many with his fists, crushing others with his mighty chest, and dealing a death blow to others with his feet.

King Ravan sent for Indrajit, his son, and said: "The streets are covered with the bodies of our dead,

fallen at the hands of this monstrous creature. Go
out, my son, and slay the foe with your magic
weapon."

Indrajit went out. And with his magic shaft he
brought Hanuman helpless to the ground. The giants
rushed to beat their foe with their fists, bound him
with ropes, and dragged him to their monarch's
feet.

Hanuman looked up at the king upon his crystal
throne. On the monarch's head his crown flashed
bright with priceless gems. About his neck hung
chains of diamonds, pearls and gold. On the mighty
upper arm of his right hand he wore the crest and
symbol of his power. And on the fingers of both
hands were rings, each one proclaiming a separate
power that lay within the monarch's hands.

The king's courtiers surrounded him; his councilors, some good and wise; and lovely women, richly
robed.

Hanuman marveled at the regal pomp and thought:
"What might and majesty this ruler grace! If only
he upheld the right and law!"

"Is this the mischiefmonger?" roared the king, his
blazing eyes upon the crouching figure.

A noble at his side replied it was, and then he
turned to Hanuman and asked: "Are you an envoy
from the God of Thunder? We know you are no

monkey, despite the form you take. Fear not, and tell us truly who you are!"

"I am no envoy of the gods," said Hanuman, "but sent by King Sugriva. Son of the God of Wind am I; and Hanuman is my name. I sought here for Rama's lady, and found her imprisoned on your isle. O King, restore her to her sorrowing husband. Else Rama and his brother will destroy you!"

"Put the wretch to death!" the king cried out.

But Ravan's brother, Vibhishan, trained in the art of soothing royal anger, said quietly: "My gracious lord! Revoke this fierce decree! Kings do not break the ancient law which forbids their slaying envoys sent them!"

Angrily the king replied: "Shall not the Vanar be punished for the evil that he's done?"

"It is lawful that his hand be maimed; and we may brand the mark of shame upon him."

King Ravan approved his brother's counsel: "Your words are true and wise. But for his crime we must invent a fitting punishment. His tail the monkey prizes most. Then set his tail on fire. And thus disgraced, return him to his king."

The court laughed and applauded the judgment of the king. At once the eager attendants brought strips of cotton soaked in oil and these they wound tightly round the monkey's tail. The drums rolled out; the tail was set afire; and Hanuman was freed to run.

Like lightning in a midnight sky, the red flames of his tail blazed though the air; and then the envoy disappeared from view.

Far off, beside a quiet stream, Hanuman alighted. He fashioned branches into a great torch, and lit it by the painful flame he carried with him. Then at the last he dipped his tail into the stream and found relief from his great agony.

Again Hanuman made his way toward Lanka, a blazing torch within his hand.

The crowds who had jeered at the monkey with his burning tail, soon saw a pall of smoke and flames rise from their city. Great walls began to reel and fall; and helpless people shrieked despairingly as they tried to stay the fire that spread to every part of Lanka.

Hanuman eyed the town he had laid in ruins; then turned and leaped across the sea whence he had come.

Hanuman Returns

The Vanar host heard Hanuman's triumphant shout as he came rushing over the rolling waters. Joyously they pressed around him, knowing that success had

crowned his toil. They brought him of their woodland fruits and shouted in their mad delight.

To King Sugriva, Hanuman said: "My eyes have
seen the fair daughter of Janaka!"

To Rama, Hanuman gave the gem Sita had taken
from her hair, and said: "This precious stone she sent
to comfort you while she dulls her woe by gazing on
your ring."

Rama pressed the treasured jewel to his breast
and spoke:

"O say, dear friend, where, where is she? Tell me

each word that fell from her sweet lips. What message did my loved one send? Ah, woe, to see this gem and ask, Where, where is she?"

(And so ends the fifth book of the Ramayana, known as the Sundara-kanda, which means The Beautiful Section.)

VI
The War at Lanka
(Lanka-kanda)

The March to the Sea

RAMA STOOD disconsolate beside the king, Sugriva. The tides of joy receded, and a flood of despair engulfed him.

"Hanuman, Son of the Wind, could leap across the sea to Lanka," he said sadly. "But how shall we and your great legions cross the leagues of treacherous water to the isle of the giant king?"

"Your noble nature should spurn grief, which can weaken the noblest enterprise," the king replied. "Who is there in the triple world to equal you in combat? Believe only in victory; trust in the mighty allies pledged to your just cause; and your arms shall once more enfold your heart's desire."

The words of the king revived Rama's spirit. Hopeful once more he turned to Hanuman and asked: "Can you, whose feet have trod the stones of every street of Lanka, describe to me the walls, the moats, the guarded ports and castles where the giants dwell?"

And Hanuman described the vastness of the city; its high walls and massive gates; its wide ramparts manned by guards with arrows, rocks, and maces, iron-headed, which could strike down a hundred dead at every blow. He told of the palace and the towers and the castles within the walls; and he described the deep moats, monster-infested, that encircled the walls without. Most eloquently he described the courage of the fierce giant warriors.

When he finished, Rama exclaimed exultantly: "The greater their strength, the prouder our victory! Soon that city of evil shall be destroyed. Go, Son of the Wind, and gather the Vanar host. And we will start on our march to the southern coast!"

Swiftly the Vanar chieftains began to assemble under Hanuman and Sugriva. From mountain heights, from sunny valleys, from forest depths monkey and bear warriors came, myriads and myriads of them, fierce and terrifying as the billows of a stormy sea. On nimble feet, in rapid strides they marched, joyously ready for the fight, their blended voices ringing out: "King Ravan and his fiends shall die!" And as the many legions flowed together, they covered the land like engulfing waves of a sea.

They passed over meadows and through forests;

they crossed streams and swarmed over mountain ranges. And always, honoring Rama's command, the marching armies avoided all towns or other haunts of men; sleeping in the open and eating of the abundant fruit and honey.

With zeal and pride they pressed forward, the earth becoming veiled and the sunbeams growing pale under the thick clouds of dust rising from the feet of the marching legions.

On and on the great army of bears and monkeys rolled southward, until they were stopped by the shores of the sea.

Ravan's Alarm

While Prince Rama, on the mainland, pondered how to bridge the waters, King Ravan, on the Isle of the Tigers, angrily viewed the havoc wrought in the city by the monkey envoy. Then the king called together his lords and addressed them:

"There are three kinds of rulers in the world. There is the ruler who plans alone when danger threatens and defies fate by scorning all delay. Then there is the ruler who gathers loyal kin, or those whose hopes are bound with his, and tries to triumph with their help. The third ruler consults his councilors for every possible approach and considers well each gain or loss, each right or wrong, and acts when all at last agree."

"Well spoken!" applauded the ministers.

"The monkey spy has long departed, leaving ruins in our city, red with the blood of many of our brave men," the king went on. "He has surely reached Rama and Sugriva, and at this very moment they may be marching toward us with thousands of their wild allies. If one Vanar could create so much havoc, how much more destructive their power will be if many succeed in crossing to the island! Ponder well, and give me your council."

One minister lifted his joined palms in reverence and said smilingly: "Are you not he who killed the Serpent God and overthrew the God of Riches? Was it not you who encountered the God of Death bearing his murderous mace, and yet survived? And is there anyone in the Three Worlds who dares to threaten you without suffering disaster? Then let Rama and Sugriva come, and leave this easy fight to be won by Prince Indrajit, your illustrious son, whose magic weapon throws a noose around the enemy's neck and drags him helpless through the dust!"

One minister after another spoke in scorn of the foe and in support of the first speaker. One wished Hanuman would return so that he, with his own sword, could cleave the head from the impudent monkey's shoulders. Another promised that if the Vanars reached Lanka, they would be scattered, like dry leaves in a screaming hurricane, until they all drowned in the angry sea. Still another brandished a mace with gore-stained spikes and implored the king and the fates for a chance to encounter Rama, Lakshman and Sugriva, so that he could crush their heads with his deadly weapon.

The Lord of War said: "Incline your ear, O Mighty King, and hear these words of mine! Let us prepare a host disguised as Kosala warriors, and they will join Rama saying that his brother Bharat sent them to his aid. And when his confidence is won, they will fall upon him and his allies and destroy them all before they ever come to Lanka."

A score of ministers spoke in turn, each skillfully repeating the confidence of the others, each trying to encourage and to placate the king.

At last the king turned to Vibhishan, his brother. "Younger brother, why has not your voice been raised in council?"

"I feared my words might displease you, O my King, if spoken here where all can hear."

"Speak!" commanded Ravan.

"O King, since that day you brought the captive, Sita, into your palace, the sacred fires have dimmed, and evil omens have appeared. I fear that Sita is as dangerous as she is fair. I beg of you to let her go. Restore the captive to her lord, before that warrior and his allies reach our land. About our city walls the hungry jackals prowl, and wolves howl for blood at every gate. I fear these omens! Let the captive go and free us from the ravages of vengeance!"

"These omens are not worthy of your fear, my brother," said the king. "Is it sinful to avenge the wrong done to a sister? Remember Surpanakha's injury by Rama's brother, and the reason for my capturing Sita!"

The wise Vibhishan replied: "That is why you captured her, but that is not the reason why you keep and woo her."

"Only a timid heart could so advise our king!" broke in the Lord of War. "Fear in a king is a disgrace, yet you would counsel him to act in fear of one lone prince, his brother, and their monkey friends!"

"O Chieftain," answered the wise Vibhishan, "when you mock Rama recall the fate of our brave Khara and his army. Nor should you forget the devastation of our city, wrought by a single member of the monkey race. Ruin will be the lot of our king, our land and people, if millions of Hanuman's kind invade our isle. So I advise: Return Sita to her wedded husband, and thus avert the danger that impends!"

In the pride and rashness of his youth, Prince Indrajit retorted:

"Fear is unknown among the members of our clan! Match even the weaklings of our race, one to ten, not with monkeys but with mighty men, and victory would still be ours!"

The king, too, angrily reproved his brother. "Were all the gods to join Rama in the fight, I still would not free Sita!"

"You do not wish to hear the truth," said Vibhishan, "and your anger proves it."

The haughty king repelled his brother's counsel, and in his anger banished Vibhishan, and warned him to flee.

Then Ravan told his ministers to ready the fourfold armies for battle and send a spy to learn the plans of the enemy.

The Spy's Report

Under cover of night the spy sent by the giants assumed the form of a mighty bird. He flew to the distant shore where Rama and Sugriva and their legions were encamped. There in a treetop he remained for days, seeing but unseen, hearing but unheard, carefully recording in his mind the information sought by Ravan. Then he returned to Lanka.

"Your brother Vibhishan," the spy reported to the king, "crossed the sea with four of his men and went at once to the enemy's camp. He told them of his banishment and offered aid to King Sugriva."

"Did the chieftains tear him apart, as the owl tears his prey?" asked one of the lords.

"Many doubted his tale," replied the spy. "But Hanuman — the same who caused such damage here — said he believed the story, just as he had in the past believed Sugriva when he was banished by his brother Bali."

"What said Sugriva?" asked the king.

"Sugriva was silent for a time when all had spoken. Then finally he said he could not trust a man who fled his brother's side when danger threatened."

"Well spoken!" exclaimed Ravan.

"But Rama came forward, looked into the face of each chieftain, and then he addressed Sugriva: 'You are a king and know the perils of a throne. This stranger of an alien race fled his brother to win our friendship, for if his brother dies he will reign in his stead. If we find he comes as foe or spy, we can strike him down with a single blow. But if his words are true, we should accept his hand as friends. He asks for shelter and, whether he is false or true, our duty commands we grant it to him.' So spoke Rama, and all the others agreed."

"How great is their army, and how strong their weapons?" asked the Lord of War.

"Their chieftains, like elephants in size, number in the thousands; and their generals, like mighty bears, number in the hundreds of thousands. Each army has millions of warriors; and, together, like a rushing tide, they spread from horizon to horizon beyond the scope of human eyes. Fierce and rough and rude are these fearless warriors. They wait restlessly for battle and hungrily for vengeance. The terrible weapons they carry match the courage of this wild forest horde."

The envoy prostrated himself, touched the ground at the king's feet with his forehead and pleaded: "Choose between your safety or Rama's queen!"

"Not if all the gods in heaven joined with all the fiends in hell against me would I yield my prize!" roared the furious king.

"However great their numbers," said the Lord of War, "they cannot cross the ocean. If they try to swim, the crocodiles and sharks and ocean serpents will feed upon them."

"Besides," said another minister, "if Sita should willingly become your queen, Your Majesty, then

Rama would leave us without engaging in battle. For no prince will fight for a faithless wife."

"But how can we accomplish that?" asked the king.

The minister leaned forward and whispered something in the monarch's ear.

A broad smile spread over Ravan's face. "Well spoken! Well spoken!" he said, nodding approvingly.

The king dismissed his council and summoned the master craftsman of the court who could present in clay or wax, in stone or wood, any image the king desired.

Sita's Lament

The mournful Sita had been refreshed by Hanuman's visit and revived by the thought that Rama must be on his way to Lanka. Her eyes sparkled with anticipation, and her pale skin glowed softly as the skin of a nectarine before it ripens. Not since the day she was carried off from the hermitage had her heart felt so light or her beauty bloomed so brilliantly.

As she sat alone in the grove a guard approached humbly and announced: "Fair lady, the royal litter waits for you!"

Then Sita was taken to the throne room where she

found the king seated upon a pillow on the floor, his head bent low in thought. He rose to greet her in seeming humility.

"I love you, Sita," he said simply. "And remember that though you have been within my court these many months, I have not forced my love upon you."

The doe-eyed queen bowed her head. "That is true, Your Majesty."

"My love for you has opened new doors to me. But one door remains closed."

"What door is that?" asked Sita softly.

"The door to paradise," replied Ravan, "the door you alone can open for me."

"Great king, no one can open that door for another. And you can do that for yourself by accomplishing three things."

"What three things are these?" the king asked suspiciously.

"Avoid war, that is the first; consider your people before yourself, that is the second," said Sita, and fell silent.

"And what is the third?" asked Ravan.

"Return me to my husband!"

"The first two I can accomplish," said the king. "But, alas, the third is no longer possible."

Sita gazed at him startled, like a woodland doe coming suddenly upon a hunter.

"Your husband Rama is dead," the king went on. "He who slew my noble Khara and his host, himself was slain in battle by my warriors."

"Where and how did my Rama die?" asked Sita in wild distress, even though she disbelieved the king.

"Permit me to spare you the details. My troops came upon your husband and his brother and their allies unawares, and slew them one and all."

"It is difficult for me to believe them taken unawares," said Sita, in bewilderment, "for I have seen Rama and Lakshman in battle. What proof have you that they are dead?"

King Ravan sent a slave to summon the magician craftsman. And the craftsman entered solemnly bearing a silver charger on which lay a head pierced by arrows, and wet with dripping blood.

"Show the lady how low in death her husband lies. Let her see the bow my troops have taken. Sita, you will now understand why I cannot send you back."

Sita's stricken eyes fixed upon the head she knew and loved so well. She saw the brow and cheek stained with blood, the eyes only half closed, the lips slightly parted as if he were about to speak. Pierced with anguish, Sita began to tremble.

"Your hopes resign, fair Sita," said the king. "Forget your dead husband, and become my queen."

"O Rama," Sita wept bitterly, "those who murdered you have murdered me! Beloved, remember your vow to keep me by your side forever! Take me to you even now!"

Then she turned fiercely to the king: "You have slain Rama and now he sleeps. Slay me with the same weapon that I, too, may sleep in death beside him! Lay our heads together, my cheek touching his, that I may die in the joy of knowing I will again be near him!"

Suddenly a messenger came from the outer court and, breathless, flung himself upon the floor in front of Ravan.

And at his whispered message, the tyrant anxiously rose. He sent word for his war council to gather, and left Sita and the court craftsman without a word to either.

The grief-stricken Sita, who had looked about in dazed surprise, turned again to the head of her dead lord. But the craftsman was gone and the head had disappeared.

"What happened to the head that was before me?" Sita asked the guard who had come to take her back to the asoka grove.

Touched by her heavy grief, the pitying guard guilelessly revealed the secret of the head upon the charger.

"Do not weep, fair Queen. Your lord, Rama, is not slain. That marvelous illusion was wrought by a great magician."

Sita's spirit absorbed the consoling words like parched earth receiving the first fresh rains. And she was comforted in the thought that despite all the tyrant king could do, Rama was alive and on his way to Lanka.

The Siege of Lanka

Rama stood upon the shore wondering how he and his allies could cross the wide ocean. His dismay turned into anger, and his anger turned into black despair. Three days in succession he was dismayed, and then angered, and then thrown into despair's dark pit. Then Rama grasped his mighty bow. He shot a stream of shafts through the air that flew so swiftly their speed set them afire. And into the billows below they fell with a mighty roar and hiss.

The sea monsters came up from the slimy depths, raising their ugly heads above the snowy foam to seek the source of their disturbance.

And the God of the Ocean appeared, chains of pearls around his great neck, his azure robes adorned with precious stones. He spoke to Rama and said:

"Prince of the Children of the Sun, heed my words: neither air nor fire, neither earth nor water can disobey their ancient laws. And I, Ocean, must remain forever unfordable. No bridge shall ever span this water. But there is one line where a causeway may be built along the hidden islands in the strait. This line has never been revealed to man. Shoot your arrow to the north, Rama, and I will reveal the spot to you."

Rama's swift arrow flew to the north and marked the line where the causeway could be built. At once the Vanars sprang to the task of gathering all the needed rocks and timber. Trees, rocks the size of autumn clouds, shrubs, bamboo and sand — mountains of each — were piled into the sea until the gaps were filled and the hundred-league causeway from shore to shore completed. Five days the Vanars labored, and when the sun sank on the fifth day, the entire stupendous task was done.

On the sixth day, the day on which Ravan tried to deceive Sita with the waxen head of Rama, the myriads of Vanars, led by Rama and his brother, and by Sugriva and Hanuman, poured across the causeway to the city of Lanka.

Tidings of the enemy reaching the outer walls of

the city was the message brought hastily to the king
at the time he sought to convince Sita of Rama's
death. And by the time the king reached the council
hall, the lords and generals were assembled.

"O faithful lords," said Ravan, "our foe has
reached the ramparts of the city. The enemy has
crossed the sea to Lanka upon a bridge. Now we shall
turn that bridge into a Bridge of Death for them,
nor leave a single one of them alive! The moment for
battle has come. Are you ready?"

"We are ready, Crown of Lanka!" the assembly
cried out.

"And you, my son Indrajit?"

"Your words, Ruler of Paradise, are music to my
ears!" the prince replied. "At your word I shall go
to lift the siege of Lanka with my magic sword!"

Ravan looked again about him over the vast assembly and he asked: "Where is Kumbhakarna, my
brother?"

"He sleeps, your majesty!"

The king smiled, and said: "He always sleeps. He
eats a mountain of food and then, for weeks or
months, he sleeps until hunger wakes him once again.
Rouse him now, for war is more pleasing to him
even than food!"

The lordly messengers of the king, afraid and
trembling, hastened to the vast chamber where the

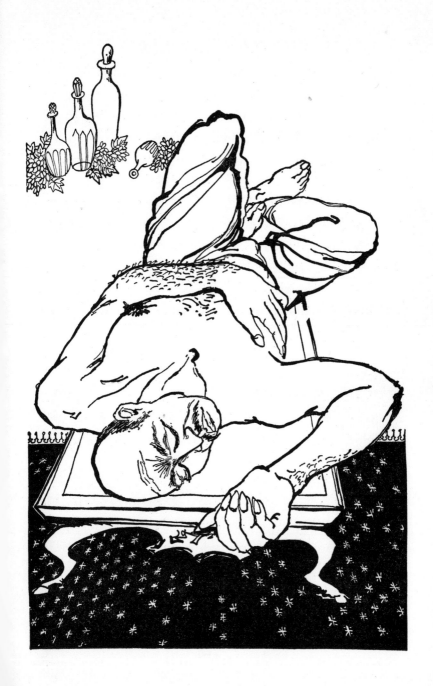

giant of a giant race lay outstretched in sleep upon a golden couch banked by fragrant flowers. Flat upon his back he lay, his stomach rising and falling like a bellows. And the great blasts of his breath flung the giant messengers to the ground like tender saplings in a gale.

They beat upon huge drums, they blew tremendous horns, and they crashed together cymbals the size of elephants' ears, creating within the vast chamber the noise of a hundred roaring lions. Still the giant did not stir.

They pounded the giant's shaggy chest with rocks and maces and huge clubs. And then, at last, they poured over Kumbhakarna's head a hundred pails of water.

The giant sat up. He shook the water out of his hair and yawned, the great jaws gaping fierce and wide. Then he opened his bloodshot eyes and demanded food. The king's messengers had come prepared. They served him enormous platters of buffalo and deer and huge beakers of wine mixed with marrow. The giant swallowed the meat in great bites and washed it down with gulps of wine, still drowsy, his slow brain beginning to form an angry question. With meat in one hand and a beaker of wine in the other, he suddenly looked around enraged.

"Why did you waken me!" he demanded. "Unless your reason is good enough, I shall break every bone in your bodies!"

"The city is besieged!" they replied in fright and sorrow.

"Who would dare do that?" asked the giant, unbelieving.

"Rama is his name. He is a prince from a distant land, and has come with his brother to challenge the king. They brought with them millions of the monkey warriors, who have vowed to slay King Ravan."

"Why?" demanded Kumbhakarna, as he went on eating.

The messengers shrugged their shoulders. "The king captured Rama's bride and brought her here to avenge the wrong to Surpanakha."

The giant rose to the height of a mighty oak. He stretched out his arms and issued a roar that shook the messengers like an earthquake and threw them to the ground. Then Kumbhakarna strode off, the messengers racing madly behind him.

The giant entered the council hall. He bowed his damp disheveled head to the king and said: "My brother, and Monarch of the World! At your word I am ready to trample underfoot the little monkeys and their vain leaders. They will be crushed like anthills under the foot of an elephant!"

"Well spoken!" said the king.

Then Ravan appointed one brave general to protect the eastern gate of the city; and another equally strong and brave to guard the southern entrance. To his son Indrajit he entrusted protection of the western approaches, and he himself undertook to guard the northern gate.

"As for you, my good brother, Kumbhakarna, we shall call upon your aid when we challenge the enemy to single combat. Then we count on you for victory. Therefore prepare yourself!"

"I am ready now!" boasted Kumbhakarna, pounding his naked chest with his fists and bursting into peals of laughter that echoed in the distant chambers like rolling drums. But his laughter suddenly ceased as the monarch frowned upon him saying: "Laughter befits victory, not the promise of victory!"

"Fear not, my brother and king!" Kumbhakarna said soberly. "Trust in my promise! Look at this, my right arm, for this arm shall lay low in the dust Sugriva and Hanuman, Rama and Lakshman, and anyone else they care to send forth."

"Each man take up his station!" ordered the king.

And all the men prepared for battle.

The Tides of War

On the tower, high above the northern gate, the tyrant Ravan appeared under the royal canopy in his warrior robe of red, decorated with ornaments of red. Fearlessly the king stood at the edge of the tower, looking down upon the place where Rama and Sugriva stood, surrounded by their men.

Sugriva shouted up to the giant king, his voice echoing against the rock of Mount Suvela:

"O King of the Giant Race! In the name of my friend Rama I challenge you to single combat, king to king!"

And as his words rang out the mighty Vanar monarch leaped up to the tower and dashed Ravan's crown from his head. But just as swiftly Ravan caught Sugriva by the shoulders, spun him round, and flung him to the ground. Before Ravan could draw another breath, Sugriva rose and stormed at Ravan's bare head with his fists. The two kings raged in furious battle, while streams of blood flowed down their limbs. Now one, now the other seemed the victor. Once Ravan caught Sugriva by the throat to fling him from the wall. But Sugriva held fast to Ravan and they both toppled down into the moat below. Up they rose along the edge, renewing their fierce combat, until, at last, feeling his strength ebbing, Sugriva leaped back to safety among his men.

Rama came up anxiously and threw his arms about his friend. "We all feared for you," he reproved sorrowfully. "Do not seek desperate adventures again. Unless counsel shows the need, leaders do not throw their lives into such danger."

Ravan had regained his place upon the tower and glared down like a wounded lion on the endless rows of Vanar warriors, sweeping toward the moat like the tides of a sea. In his ears rang the enemy's order to charge the gates and paint the earth red with the blood of the giants. Ravan's eyes blazed with fury and he commanded his men to open the gates and rush upon the enemy, cleaving the head of every Vanar from its owner's shoulders.

The troops of the giant king rushed out of the gates, and earth and sky rang with the clash of their spears. Each swing of their ax, each blow of their mace brought down a Vanar. Loud as the roar of an angry ocean, the Vanars swept up in answering attack. And the trained Lanka warriors, with their great weapons, were overwhelmed by the scorned monkeys and bears carrying uprooted oaks and huge rocks.

When the wild attack halted, there were many

killed and many more wounded on both sides, yet neither side could claim a victory.

One last attempt Rama and Sugriva made to stop the bloodshed, and sent a final message to King Ravan:

"Yield while there still is time, and bring the lady Sita within this hour!"

Ravan turned his fury upon the messenger and shouted: "Seize him! Seize the Vanar and let him die!"

Then the chiefs of each opposing side proposed to test their strength in single combat.

The fight began with Indrajit challenging Prince Angad, Bali's son. Then face to face Hanuman fought with Jambumali; and Nila with Nikumbha; and Nitraghna with Rasmiketu. These met and fought, and thousands more. And the trampled earth ran red with blood.

Now one side won, and now it lost; and neither side could claim clear victory.

The foemen struggled fiercely as night fell. And through the gloom of night the battle still raged on. In the thick dark about them the warriors could scarcely tell their friends from foes.

Throughout the days that followed, the tides of battle ebbed and flowed. Torn banners and broken swords heaped the ground about mound after mound of silent dead, and mound after mound of the suffering wounded.

King Ravan watched the bloody battle rage below, no longer scornful of a foe who fought so bravely and so well. His wounded pride made his temples pound with rage.

"Revenge!" he shouted. "I must avenge my nobles slain!"

Ravan summoned Kumbhakarna to enter the fight. In pomp and pride the giant strode through the city gate, shouting in a voice that re-echoed from the distant hills. Like an invincible tower of strength he moved toward the enemy, and when the monkey legions saw him come their way, they turned and fled in mad retreat.

They fled before him and the giant followed them.

The Vanar chieftain, Prince Angad, ordered his troops to stop their headlong flight. "Will you flee from your honor?" shouted the prince. "Even if the giant had the strength of a thousand elephants, he still is no match for our numbers!"

The Vanars paused. And then the tide of millions turned to sweep upon the monster foe. Leaping through the air and coming on all sides through the treetops, the warriors showered upon Kumbhakarna an unending rain of rocks and branches. But he neither flinched nor stopped.

With fury in his eyes, Kumbhakarna swung his mighty sword like a scythe, mowing down ten and twenty monkey warriors at a time. And wherever he caught them, there they fell like ripened grain. And the giant trampled them underfoot as he plowed his way through them.

The monkeys turned again and fled in terror. They climbed trees, escaped to high places, or hid in caves too small for the giant to follow. Again the chieftains brought them back with stinging words. Again and again their ranks broke. Again and again their ranks re-formed, and the fight went on.

Hanuman came fiercely at the monster, trying to engage him in single combat. Kumbhakarna dealt him a slashing blow on the chest, and a crimson torrent began to run down the Vanar warrior's body. Maddened by the pain, Hanuman flung himself heedlessly at the giant's face. This brave action brought to Hanuman's aid many of his followers. With bared teeth, their nails digging into the giant's flesh wherever they could attach themselves, they swept down in great waves and imprisoned their foe like a sudden avalanche, until he could move neither his hands nor his feet. They obstructed his vision; they held his nostrils so that he could not breathe.

With a sudden gasp the giant shook himself violently and his assailants fell like flies shaken off by an enraged bull. He raised his freed hands and swung his spear again.

And once again the slain piled up in mounds about him.

All day long they fought, the Vanars retreating before the giant, and returning again and again to the attack. Each of the Vanar chieftains took his turn leading the army against Kumbhakarna. And each time the giant called out for Rama.

Then Rama appeared in the path of the giant, grasping his bow. He stood firmly, calmly, as the great monster neared, the earth trembling beneath his tread. And Rama sent a torrent of deadly arrows that pierced the giant's armor, each wound in the arms and legs becoming the mouth of an ever-widening red stream. The pain of his mortal blows loosened the grip of the giant hands, and his weapons dropped to the ground. Still he plodded forward, his heavy hands killing a thousand of the foe at each stride.

Though the blood flowed down his limbs like torrents down a mountainside, Kumbhakarna lifted a huge mass of rock high above his head to fling at Rama. But the master bowman had raised his bow and placed upon it two crescent-headed arrows given him by his teacher Vishvamitra. He aimed; then let them fly. One pierced the giant's heart, the other tore

the giant's head from off his shoulders. For an eerie
moment the headless giant remained erect. Then
slowly he leaned, like a tower shaken by an earthquake, and crashed to the ground.

The fall of the mighty Kumbhakarna brought a
great shout of joy from the Vanars. Among the giants
went up a great cry of woe.

"I have lost my right arm which held off danger,"
lamented the king. "This evil day was foretold by
Vibhishan, but my foolish pride drove him away.
Now I reap the fruit of my offense. Today my life is
done. Nor can it ever bring me joy, until my matchless brother is avenged!"

A general beside the king said: "O sire, our bravest
has fought and died, and our loss is great. But I myself will go forth and sweep away the foe."

At the words of his devoted chieftain, new life and
spirit came to Ravan. And he sent fresh troops to
take up the battle once again.

The giants expected only a brief encounter, in
which the monkeys and bears would be destroyed
like an anthill. And for every giant lost in battle a
thousand monkeys were destroyed. But there were
so many of the Vanars that their great losses seemed
slight in comparison with the losses of the giants.

No longer did the people of Lanka speak with contempt of the enemy outside their gates. The women,

whose husbands or sons had been killed in battle, spoke boldly in their bitterness against the king.

Some asked: "Why does not Ravan force the captive to become his queen? Then Rama would not want her, and would leave our city."

And others answered: "Long ago the king forced his love upon a maiden, not knowing she was a nymph from heaven. She vowed that if he should ever be guilty of this again, the Storm God himself would seek vengeance of him."

"Then the king should send Sita back to her husband, or himself meet Rama in single combat," they replied.

The king was told of the complaints made by the people, and he announced angrily: "Today I shall go out to engage the foe. And this day my shafts shall feed him and his allies to the dogs and to the vultures of the air!"

Ravan's End

Ravan ascended his war chariot, drawn by eight fiery steeds. Closely behind followed the great army of royal charioteers and foot soldiers without number. As the king passed through the streets of Lanka at the head of his army, his golden armor flashing in the sun, the gathered throngs sent up great shouts of joy.

"Our king will crush the foe beneath his feet!" they assured each other.

"Long live our king!" they shouted.

As Ravan's chariot dashed through the wide-flung city gates, he cried out furiously: "This day shall bring the Vanars' end. And on this day I'll tear up by its roots the tree, Rama, and win its lovely fruit, the lady Sita!"

The earth shook under Ravan's chariot. And over brook and hill and grove, beneath his rain of arrows, the Vanars fell or fled.

Close upon the king's car came the deafening thud of chariots, drawn by three million elephants; and an army four times that number, mounted on fiery steeds. In one short hour behind Raven's host the plain was spread with bleeding limbs and mountains of the dead and dying.

From his swift car the king shouted to his troops, and all the while his eyes roved to discover his prized target, Rama. And Rama, on his side, listened intently through the clangor of battle and peered through the dust-filled air for the sight of his enemy, Ravan.

In the moment Rama caught sight of his approaching foe, he strained his sounding bow. And to its awful clang the region roundabout re-echoed. Rama recalled all that he had learned from Vishvamitra, and called to his aid the mystic power of *Bala* and *Atibala*. At last he bent his bow. And through the air an arrowy tempest poured on Ravan. Some of the unloosed shafts hissed like snakes; and some appeared like fearful lions or pouncing tigers, and some like hungry wolves in packs.

Each shaft Ravan shot at his adversary, Rama foiled in midair, splintering the shafts and sending them back at their bowman. Ravan hurled a spear through the air that flashed like fire. But Rama deflected it from its course with a fiery dart that threw the weapon harmless to the ground.

The sky above them darkened with the missiles flying to their mark. And though Rama was able to defend himself against Ravan, he failed to wound the giant king decisively. To Rama's aid came Lakshman, his brother, and poured arrows thick as hail on Ravan's coat of mail.

The giant king cried out in scorn: "It is you I shall kill first, before I cleanse the earth of Rama!"

He flung a spear with such fury that it flickered through the air like a serpent's tongue, caught Lakshman full upon the chest, and hurled him to the ground. Rama gasped in grief, not knowing whether Lakshman had been stunned or wounded mortally.

Out of nowhere, so it seemed, Hanuman appeared. He lifted the fallen Lakshman and, in one great leap, carried him far behind the battleground. There Hanuman revived the wounded prince and healed him.

Ravan sought to wrest victory from Lakshman's fall, and he fought with awful might to overwhelm Rama. Still Rama returned arrow for arrow and blow for blow, pausing only from time to time during the long combat to praise the God of Day and pray for victory, resolved to win or die.

Rama's gleaming shafts found their mark like the fangs of deadly serpents. Yet the king betrayed no sign that he even felt their sting or that his strength was slowly seeping from him. As Ravan recklessly rushed upon his foe, determined to crush him with a single spear thrust, one of Rama's arrows pierced the king's shoulder. For an instant he stood faint, and bleeding fast. He lifted high his spiked mace and rushed again at Rama. And as he neared, Rama sent one swift shaft to the monarch's chest and pierced his heart. The giant warrior, with hand still upraised holding the heavy mace, fell forward on his face. And where he fell, there he lay dead.

When Ravan's host saw that their king had fallen they let out a yell of terror. They fled in disorder from the field of battle, throwing away their weapons as they ran. And upon them rushed the joyous

Vanars; pursuing them to the city gates; pelting them with sticks and stones, while they shouted their praise of Rama.

Only Vibhishan, Ravan's brother, did not rejoice. He sank down beside the still body of his brother and mourned: "O hero brother! O brother, bold and overbold, whom pride forbade to listen to the fate foretold! Fallen is the royal tree! The beacon fire is dead and cold!"

Rama came near to console him and said: "Restrain your grief and pay to the brave dead the dues that yet remain. All enmity ends at the Gates of Death! Your warrior king died nobly!"

Rama thrust his mighty arrows into the ground to form a bier and upon it they lifted the fallen king.

Then the dead monarch was carried into Lanka in a vast procession, moving slowly to the sad measures of a dirge.

They brought the dead hero to his lovely queen, Mandodari, and left him there alone. Her tear-dimmed eyes gazed mournfully upon the monarch, and she wailed:

"Your love for Sita brought you death, and me it brought a sea of woe!"

Outside the city walls Rama urged the king's brother to prepare the rites due the royal dead. At first Vibhishan opposed using certain sacred rites because the dead king had incensed the gods by abducting another man's wife.

But Rama replied: "Though he scorned the right, yet his dauntless heart and deeds of valor have earned for him the honors due the slain!"

The sacred fire was brought from the royal palace; and with it sandalwood, and fragrant scents, and ornaments of pearl and coral. And on a golden litter, they brought the warrior king, covered with pennants and with flowery wreaths. The offerings to the dead were paid; the oil and clotted milk were shed; and then, as high on a deerskin coverlet the body of the king was set upon the pyre, they strewed parched grain upon the dead and Vibhishan set the sacred kindling fire to the piled sandal logs: all sacred rites performed as the rules ordained.

When the last remains of the giant Ravan were turned into ashes upon the pyre, Rama, with his brother Lakshman at his right and King Sugriva at his left, announced that Vibhishan would take his brother's place upon the throne.

The people, grateful that the conqueror had no designs upon their kingdom, prepared solemnly for the coronation.

Then Rama, his task of warrior done, unstrung his deadly bow and laid aside his glittering shafts.

Sita's Triumph

Hanuman left the camp outside Lanka and sped into the city, racing from street to street and leaping from tree to tree, bearing a message to Sita from Rama.

He found Sita in the lovely garden, seated beneath a tree. Her beautiful hair lay in tangled strands about her, and down her pale cheeks flowed rivulets of tears.

"Fair queen," he hailed her, "put off your grief! The task is done! The foe is slain! The war is won! Your Rama, triumphant, has sent me to you, because his vow will not permit him to enter a city. But King Vibhishan rules now in Ravan's place, and you are safe. Your Rama sends his word to you: 'My love, weep no more, for all is well!'"

Through her sobs of rapturous joy, Sita thanked Hanuman: "More precious than gems and gold, the message you have brought!"

"Permit me, before we leave here," said Hanuman, glancing at the huddled group of guards about her, "permit me to slay these creatures who have treated you so cruelly."

"Do not harm them," pleaded Sita. "The fault is not theirs. They are but servants, who must obey their king's commands."

"Your words reflect your noble nature," said Hanuman in admiration.

"My first and only wish is to reach Rama's side!"

Sita, now radiant, prepared for the journey to Rama, and soon she appeared, her hair smooth and shining about the lovely head, her raiment sweet with fragrant scents and gay with ornaments. But a veil of pensiveness fell over her as she entered the silken-screened litter awaiting her outside Lanka's northern gate.

As the queen was borne along the plain, great crowds of Vanars pressed close, struggling to catch a glimpse of the fair one for whom the great Ravan had met his death in battle.

At King Vibhishan's command the pressing crowds were hurled back, and they responded with a wild roar.

Rama, moved to anger at this, reproved the king: "I count these people as my own. Why do you vex them with your threats? A woman's conduct is her best defense. And she, my queen, may cease to hide her face a while, for is not her husband at her side? Put down the litter, and let Sita come to meet me, while the woodland warriors gaze upon her face."

Disturbed and anxious, Sita left the litter and walked slowly toward her husband, doubt and fear

struggling in her wistful eyes. Then, suddenly forget-
ful of the crowds about her, her face bright as the
moon without a cloud, her trusting eyes looked lov-
ingly at Rama.

He looked tenderly upon her face as she stood
trembling by his side. Yet as he spoke his voice was
harsh and terrible his words: "Lady, my task is
done! With this arm I cleansed dishonor from my
name! And you, the prize of war, are free again. But
you must know it was not my love for you that led
me to this isle. I fought for the cause of honor, and to
uphold the law of right. And while I fought you
dwelt in Ravan's court and he, at will, could take
you in his arms. Before you lies the world and in it
you may freely go wherever you may wish. But to
my home I cannot bring the one who dwelt in Ravan's bower."

Each word of Rama, like a poisoned dart, pierced
Sita's heart. Choking with tears, she replied: "Can
you, a prince, to me, a princess, speak such words?
The meanest hind would find them more befitting. All
my past life cries out against your cruel words! If I
lay helpless, seized in Ravan's hated arms, put your
blame upon the robber, and my unhappy fate, but do
not blame the dove for touching the hawk's talons.
Is all my faithful love forgotten? If I had known
your sentence of rejection, I would have had you

shun the fruitless strife, and for myself sought sweet relief in death!"

Quickly she turned to Lakshman and said: "I will not live to bear this shame! Best and truest friend, prepare a pyre for me and I will seek in its bright flames a refuge for my black despair!"

Lakshman looked pleadingly at his brother. But Rama sternly gazed before him, showing no pity for the weeping queen. And not a chieftain among all the thousands round him dared pray, or question, or advise.

At last the wood was piled, the fire was lit, and gentle Sita humbly prayed: "O Lord of Flame! My universal witness be against this charge. Hear, and aid Sita! Protect my body on the pyre!"

Fearless to the last, the crowds saw her in her gay attire within the fury of the fire, and from them all went up a piercing cry.

The great cry shrilled through Rama's ears as his tear-filled eyes turned toward heaven. And there before him he saw the Lord Brahma, by whose command the worlds were created, and heard him say:

"O Rama! How can you, incarnation of Vishnu the Creator, suffer your queen to brave the pyre? You, to whom all creatures bow, do you not recognize your heavenly nature, that you treat Janaka's daughter as would a mortal man?"

"I am a mortal at this time, and son of a great king. If my queen were not tried by fire, slander would forever cast its shadow on her name. The Lord of Flame protect her! For my heart knows she is innocent of all blame!"

The circling flames rolled swiftly backward from the pyre. And there was Sita, fair as the morning sun, arrayed in royal crimson robes, her glistening coils of hair entwined with gems. And as she walked toward Rama, he heard the Lord of Fire call out: "Behold your queen, without blot or blemish!"

Rama clasped her in his arms and cried out with tears of joy: "Now you are mine again! Upon your pure fame no shadow lies! Your faithful heart has been made clear to all the many thousands here! As heroes cling fast to their glory, so will I cling fast forever to my beloved!"

On his breast the gentle Sita hid her glowing face.

Return to Ayodhya

King Vibhishan came out of the city to visit Rama and his companions, and he said:

"Your fourteen years of exile are drawing to an end. Soon you will be free to enter the city. And when you do, attendants will await you with brimming urns of precious oils and scents to rest you; and nothing that your heart desires shall be denied you!"

"All such delights I cannot heed," replied Rama graciously. "For I must turn back toward home where my brother, faithful Bharat, anxiously awaits me. I long to see my native land and, alas, the way to it is far, and over difficult, dreary roads."

"A single day will bring you there, my friend," said Vibhishan. "I have a magic chariot that will take you through the air like a bird, and carry you to your native land, unwearied, in one day. This is the chariot Ravan seized from the God of Gold, and in this chariot he brought Sita here. Then take a little time to rest as honored guest within my halls."

"O best of giant kind, I yearn to see my home and kin. Forgive my heart, that cannot brook delay, and speed me on my way!"

The magic car, flashing and blazing in the sun, was brought to Rama. Vibhishan stood beside it and said humbly: "O Rama, behold, your will is mine!"

Rama and Sita took their places in the chariot, and Lakshman stood beside them with his bow still in his hand. Then Rama called out: "O Vanar chiefs! Farewell! Your aid brought to a noble end the task begun in fear and doubt. And now toward home retrace your steps. Brave warriors, farewell! My last farewell!"

Then said Sugriva: "Before I hasten homeward it

is my dearest wish to pay my homage to you in beautiful Ayodhya!"

"That is my wish as well," said Vibhishan.

And Hanuman cried out: "I, too, would go with you!"

"Ascend, my faithful friends!" said Rama.

As the magic car began to rise from the ground, the Vanar king, the king of the Giant Race, and faithful Hanuman sprang to Rama's side. The wondrous car rose toward the clouds like a silver bird, and from the multitude below a great shout went up: "Rama! Rama! Rama!"

As they sped through the sky Rama pointed out to Sita the battlefields: "Love, there the giant hosts and Vanars met." Then he pointed out the causeway built across the ocean; the shore where they had camped, not knowing how to cross the waters. "There, darling of my soul, we toiled in sight of the unconquered sea."

Sita, in turn, showed Rama the landmarks of the torturous trip when she was carried from the hermitage to Lanka. Then both of them, joined by Lakshman, showed their guests the road on which they traveled from the royal city to the Forest of Panchavati, excepting that the places were indicated backwards.

"There! There!" cried Rama, "The spires of our

city! Ayodhya! Our home! Our long-lost home!"

In reverent silence they brought the magic car down outside the city gates.

Then Rama spoke privately to Hanuman before sending him to Bharat, announcing the return of the exiles:

"Mark carefully the grief or joy on Bharat's face. Mark every gesture, look and attitude. For where is the heart that can resign a kingdom? And if my brother Bharat thirsts to reign, won by the years of power within his hands, return quickly here to me and tell me of his feelings."

But Bharat received Hanuman's message with great rapture. And he sent Satrughna to prepare a royal welcome.

The shrines of the city were decked in flowers; incense was lit on every altar and, like a sudden fragrance, the air was filled with music. In festive robes, the nobles rode out upon their jewel-bedecked elephants; and close behind followed a thousand chiefs upon their mounts; while still another thousand drove in glittering chariots. On foot came countless hosts, and in the silk-screened litters rode the ladies of the court. Above the shouts of joy, the drums, the shells and tambours, rose the happy cry from countless throats: "Rama! Rama! Rama!"

At the head of the procession a solemn royal attendant bore a golden footstool, upon which rested Rama's golden sandals. During all the years of his exile, these had served as a symbol of Rama's throne. Behind the sandals rode exultant Bharat.

At last they came out to the place where they saw the two brothers standing at each side of Sita.

" 'Tis he! 'Tis Rama!" went up the cry.

Bharat was first to dismount and approach. He raised his hands, palm to palm, and bowed low. Then he knelt reverently before his brother. Rama quickly lifted him and held him in a brotherly embrace.

As Satrughna and the royal ladies, each in turn, came forward, the throngs sang out:

"Rama! Rama! Ramachandra!"

Bharat put the golden sandals upon Rama's feet, saying in a voice that all could hear: "On this glad day I restore to you the realm of the Kosalas. Begin your royal task, O King! The strain, too great for my feeble arm, will be light as a feather for you. Grant your glorious rule to your people, after their long patience with me!"

The faithful love of the brother moved all hearts, and happy tears were shed as Rama once again embraced the loyal Bharat.

Then silence fell as Rama stood with bent head, and a moon-white canopy was brought by four carriers and held above him, shielding from all eyes the age-old rite, consecrating the new monarch with sacred oil.

At last the rite was over. King Rama and Queen Sita were escorted to the palace; and the month-long feast of the coronation began.

Rama gave princely gifts to all his devoted friends. And to his queen he presented a matchless string of pearls. Sita let the softly shimmering gems rest about her neck a moment, then she gently took them off and held them in her hand, her eyes questioning Rama.

Rama, understanding her silent wish, smiled and said: "Yes, love, bestow the gems on that good friend, faithful through toil and peril to the end." And he smiled again to see Sita's pearls hang on Hanuman's bosom, like a moonlit cloud encircling a hill.

Homeward went the two kings, Sugriva and Vibhishan, in the magic chariot, and each returned to his throne and duties. But Hanuman remained in Ayodhya. For both Rama and Sita implored him to remain forever by their side; and Hanuman, son of the Wind God, had no wish to leave them.

O Happy Days!

King Rama changed the name of Ayodhya to "The City of Victory." "I have fought against evil in the

form of Ravan," said he, "therefore let my city be named in honor of the triumph of good over evil."

Through the ten thousand years of Rama's rule, the realm was blessed with peace; the flocks increased; the harvests never failed; crime and want were unknown; and no house was ever desolate.

So calm, so happy was that time.

And the rule of Rama is forever remembered as *Ramaraja,* which simply means "in the days of Rama's rule." But the word has an added meaning, now as then. People say "Ramaraja," and they sigh wistfully. For to them it means "that golden age when Rama ruled" — or "those happy days!"

Were Valmiki born again today, so they say in India, and were he to seek a theme for a great epic, he would retire to a distant hermitage and write once again the Ramayana.

(And so ends the sixth book of the Ramayana, known as the Yuddha-kanda or Lanka-kanda, which means The War Section or the Lanka Section. The sixth book ends with the following assurance:

"They who hear this poem which Valmiki made shall obtain all their desires and all their prayers shall be fulfilled.")

VII
The Book That Was Added
(Uttara-kanda)

The Work of the Rhapsodists

THERE IS every reason to believe that the original Ramayana began with the banishment of Rama and Sita and ended with their triumphant return home, told as a romantic and deeply moving story devoid of supernatural beings and events. Then a remarkable poet, three or four or five thousand years ago, selected this well-known theme, of great antiquity even in his day, and made it the vehicle of an epic which gave full range to his talent and imagination.

In his work the poet explored nearly every basic human emotion, from love and self-sacrifice to lust and despair; from bitterness in defeat to humiliation in victory. In addition, he poured into his poem his deep love for every aspect of nature. He never tired of describing the forests and streams, the wild inhabitants of the wilderness, and the ecstatic joys of living close to Mother Earth — joys he felt were greater than those to be had living in the royal palaces of even such romantic and glittering cities as Ayodhya, Kishkindha and Lanka. Though the rapturous nature descriptions are numerous, they never impede the development of the main characters in the story, nor do they impede the progress of the tender love story.

Naturally, this epic was often repeated and long remembered. And quite as naturally enthusiastic admirers (called Rhapsodists) began to embellish it with details of their own imagining, since the epic was preserved by word of mouth. But, alas, the enthusiasm of some of the poet's admirers was greater than their talent. And the epic became cluttered with demons and evil spirits, vindictive nymphs and pious seers, performing magical deeds. Many legends and genealogies were added here and there by the latter-day Rhapsodists, always with good motives but not always in good taste.

It is believed that the entire first book of the Ramayana — seventy-seven cantos or chapters dealing with Rama's Youth — was a later addition. Certainly the opening four chapters which tell how Valmiki became an epic poet could not have been in the original epic. It is a folk legend invented to explain the origin of the Ramayana. Unlike many other parts and legends interpolated into the work, the opening legend is full of charm. This is what it tells:

The Story of Valmiki

Long ago there was a highway robber who lived in a certain forest and like a jackal pounced upon defenseless travelers, taking from them whatever they possessed.

One day several holy men came by, each carrying in his hand the cup of the hermit beggar, and the robber demanded that they give up whatever they had of value.

"Let us pass," the holy men pleaded. "You can see we are hermits who have renounced the world. What could we have that would be of value to such as you?"

"If you have nothing of value," argued the robber, "you do not deserve to live."

"Of course we have something of value," the holy men replied, offended. "But what is valuable to us will be of no value to you. For we value most spiritual truth."

"What is spiritual truth good for?" demanded the thief.

"If you have enough of it," they replied, "the gods will grant you whatever you desire."

"Is it difficult to acquire spiritual truth?" asked the thief suspiciously.

"No, not at all," said the holy men. "We will teach you the secret precept, which consists of repeating one short word, inaudibly. The longer you repeat it without interruption, the greater your acquisition of spiritual truth."

"What is the word?" asked the robber.

"Rama, said backwards," they replied. "Just sit down and repeat 'Amar — amar — amar — amar,' as if it were a sacred hymn."

The robber let the holy men pass, seated himself on the ground as soon as they had left, and repeated the secret precept in his mind, without a movement of his lips.

Days and weeks and months and years passed. The robber remained in the same spot, inaudibly repeating the word, to acquire more and more spiritual truth. As the seasons passed in cycle after cycle, the ants of the forest built their anthill about him. Still he continued his silent chant of "Amar — amar — amar."

After a thousand years had passed, a group of holy men came through the forest and noticed a man inside a gigantic anthill. They released him from it and asked his name. He no longer remembered it. So they named him Valmiki, which means Anthill. The robber-turned-anthill had acquired spiritual truth and a state of holiness so great that he could ask the gods for anything he wished and it would be granted him. But by this time Valmiki was no longer interested in worldly treasure. He addressed himself to Narada, son of Brahma the Creator, and said:

"Tell me, O sainted Narada, Prince of those whose lore in words of wisdom flows, tell me who is the wisest, the bravest, the best of men in all the world, so noble in might, so gentle in skill, that he can guard the Three Worlds from all ill?"

"His name is Rama, and when he ruled on earth his people feared no evil," replied Narada, God of Words and Wisdom, before whose clear eyes lie the past, the present and the future.

"Tell me about Rama," urged Valmiki.

"He is as powerful as the God Vishnu; lovely as Chandra, Lord of the Night; patient and gentle as Mother Earth; but when angered, he is as fierce and world-destroying as the God of Fire. And in his person he is the embodiment of Justice."

"Tell me more about him," begged Valmiki.

And Narada related the story of Rama from the beginning until the very end, with Rama's Ascent to Heaven.

Valmiki was deeply stirred. "Would that I could write down in verse all I have heard this day," he sighed. "But, alas, I have not the gift of poetry."

One day, as Valmiki came out from the Sacred

River and walked toward a grove of mango trees to refresh himself with their fruit, he noticed two birds on a branch, so lovely and so loving that they reminded him of Rama and Sita in Narada's story. Suddenly an arrow came flying through the air and pierced one of the birds, wounding it fatally, as the other, startled and bereaved, rose on his wings and filled the air with his grief and despair.

Valmiki turned angrily to find the unseen hunter who had thoughtlessly destroyed a creature which could be of no value to him. He cried out:

> "No fame be thine for endless time,
> Because, base outcast, of thy crime,
> Whose cruel hand was fain to slay
> One of this gentle pair at play!"

At that moment, so the legend goes, Brahma appeared before the hermit and commanded him to record in song The Adventures of Rama and Sita, using rhyming verses similar to those he had just used expressing his anger at the cruel hunter. And Brahma the Creator, Lord Most High, promised that the poem would be deathless, saying:

> "As long as in this firm-set land
> The streams shall flow, the mountains stand,
> So long throughout the world, be sure,
> The great Ramayana shall endure."

The Story Goes On

The Ramayana really ends with the sixth book and
the Rule of Rama in the Golden Age. But many centuries later another book was added by the Rhapsodists. This part they frankly named the Uttara-kanda,
or The Added Section, though still claiming that it
was written by Valmiki.

After long and tedious digressions about events
happening ages before the days of Rama, and about
characters only remotely related to the characters in
the Ramayana, we finally come to the following
very strange account:

Though at the end of the sixth book we are told
that throughout the long rule of Rama

> "Unknown were want, disease and crime,
>   So calm, so happy was the time,"

we are suddenly told of people coming to their king,
complaining:

"There is want and poverty in our land, O Ma-
haraja!"

"Where does it come from?" asked Rama.

"We are being punished for a sin committed in our
midst," they replied.

"What sin is that?" asked the king.

"The sin of your taking Sita back after she had spent so long a time in Ravan's Court of Women."

Rama's face darkened with sorrow. He told them how Sita had passed through the Trial of Fire to prove her innocence of all blame.

But the people only sighed and repeated: "We are being punished by hunger in our land because of a sin!"

Through the kingdom of the Kosalas rumors began to fly, and though Rama knew his wife was pure as the newly fallen snow on the highest peak of the Himalaya Mountains, he could not ignore the discontent among his people.

As Rama and Sita sat in their garden at sunset one day, watching the shadows lengthen, Sita said reflectively: "Do you remember, my lord, the twilight hours in the forests of Chitrakuta during the first days of our exile? How I long sometimes to visit those quiet places and the holy hermits who dwell there in peace!"

Rama remained silent for a time, then said: "You shall have your wish. I shall ask Lakshman to take you to the Chitrakuta Forest tomorrow."

The following day, Queen Sita, accompanied only by Prince Lakshman, left the City of Victory and rode out to the lonely forest. When they reached

Chitrakuta, Lakshman painfully explained to the queen the unrest in the kingdom and the rumors in the land.

"Your face tells me you have evil tidings," said Sita.

Lakshman bowed his head low as he told Sita of the king's order to take her to the forest and tell her there of her banishment. And he ended, saying:

"It is not the wish of the king, but of the people who forever blame their own adversity on the sins of others."

At first Sita was stunned. Then, as the bitter tears rolled down her cheeks, she said: "You know how long the king and I have prayed for a son! Now I am with child. I was about to tell the king. Yet now, I beseech you not to tell him. Though how I dread to bear my child in this wilderness!"

"Near here the sage Valmiki dwells," said Lakshman. "Seek him and the good seer will care for you."

When Lakshman slowly turned and left her, Sita started wearily in search of Valmiki's hermitage. She lost her way and wandered for days, her clothes in tatters, her feet blistered and torn by brambles; and in her heart the painful thought of her unjust banishment festered like an open wound. Hungry and parched she moved on hopelessly, until the very birds of the air took pity and fanned her with their wings to keep her from fainting. And a great black tiger followed her at a respectful distance to protect her from the hungry wolves.

One day she saw a cottage in the depth of the forest and she ran toward it. But her strength was gone and she fell to the ground. The kindly old Valmiki found her there and carried her to his home and placed her in the care of his noble wife.

That night Sita gave birth to twin boys and named them Lava and Kusa.

Though the wound of her separation from Rama never healed, the joy of her two growing sons was a balm for her sorrow.

Twenty years later word reached Valmiki that King Rama was offering the Horse Sacrifice, to which all the great sages were invited, with Valmiki among them. The sage took his two pupils, the twins, with him to the royal palace. And there the boys chanted the poem Valmiki had taught them. They repeated twenty cantos each day, on twenty-five successive days, until all five hundred cantos of the great epic were recited.

"Who are you?" asked the astonished king.

"Our mother's name is Sita," said Lava and Kusa. "But our father's name we do not know."

The king begged Valmiki to bring Sita back to

him; and he explained how he had yearned for her through all the lonely years.

By royal decree a great assemblage gathered to witness Sita's return. And when she appeared, wearing ornaments and garlands given to her by the saintly Anasuya, shouts of joy and admiration went up from the crowds, for their queen was as radiantly beautiful as she had been upon her wedding day.

The king rose to greet her, and to his people he proclaimed as she drew near:

"Never in the heart of Rama was there any doubt of Sita's faithfulness. Long ago the God of Fire attested to her virtue. But my subjects were not content. Bowing to their wishes, I banished Sita from her home. Now she returns. And before your eyes, and the eyes of all the gods, I command her to prove once more, by trial, her innocence and virtue, so that none may ever cast a doubt on her again!"

Sita listened to his words with downcast eyes and heavy heart. She did not plead her innocence as she had pleaded long ago in Lanka. Nor did she invoke the gods to protect her. In a voice as clear as the water of a mountain stream in spring, Sita called out:

"O Mother Earth Divine! If unstained in thought and action I have lived all the days of my life, and you find no fault with me, spare me this shame and take me back, you who gave me birth!"

Her words frightened King Rama and all the people about him. Then terror struck them as they saw the earth open up before their eyes. Out of the abyss rose a splendid throne set with rubies and adorned with gold, upon it bearing the Goddess of Earth in a robe of flowing silver.

"My Sita," said the Goddess of Earth, "I have come to take you with me to the Land of Happiness."

A shower of flowers descended from heaven as Sita took her place upon the throne beside the goddess. Then Queen Sita and the goddess disappeared, swallowed up by the earth that closed over them.

Ever since that time the song that echoes through the crags of the Himalayas and whose cadence is carried on the waves of the Ganges River is the song in praise of the beautiful Sita; of her joys and sorrows, of her faithfulness to Rama; and how, in the end, she returned to Mother Earth.

(And so ends the seventh book of the Ramayana, called the Uttara-kanda, which means The Section That Was Added.)

And so ends the story of The Adventures of Rama.

The Ram Lila

IN THE AUTUMN of the year, when the days grow short and the nights grow long, a ten-day festival is held in practically every town and hamlet in the land of the Hindus. The celebration is observed in different ways in different parts of India; but everywhere it is a very joyous festival.

For weeks before the arrival of the holiday, boys and men wander through the market places dressed up as monkeys or bears, preceded by loud drummers. And everyone knows that they are out collecting funds for costumes, fireworks, and effigies to be used in the Ram Lila, which means The Drama of Rama.

Everywhere people prepare for the Ram Lila, in which nearly everyone takes part. Costumes, mostly of monkeys and demons, trolls and baboons, bears and apes — like the costumes of Hallowe'en — are taken out to be repaired and decorated anew. Carriages are ornamented with tinsel and paper flowers. Two huge wooden horses on immense platforms, kept in storage the year round, are rolled out to be repainted brilliant white with patches of blood red.

And two awesome effigies are made of bamboo, sometimes rising to thirty or even fifty feet in height. The bamboo frames are filled with firecrackers and then the effigies are covered with strips of bright-colored paper of different sizes.

Early on the first morning of the festival the two wooden horses are rolled into the center of the clearing chosen to serve as stage. Yet already the stage is surrounded by a crowd of onlookers dressed in their holiday best; the women gay in red and yellow silks, ornamented with tinkling silver jewelry. All about are the young boys, wearing fox-nosed monkey masks and monkey costumes, their long upright tails bobbing behind them as they dash about excitedly, watching for the arrival of the actors chosen to take the parts of Rama and his beloved brother, Lakshman.

Hawkers wander through the patient crowds selling sweets as the great clearing fills with musicians, dancers and actors dressed as demons or monkeys, or dressed as soldiers, carrying swords and firecrackers made to look like bombs. Suddenly a cry goes up, and everyone turns to view the approaching procession of principal actors born aloft on litters, or drawn in resplendent carriages such as one sees in circuses, or on richly decorated elephants. Chief among the arrivals are two youths whose faces have been painted with yellow turmeric. One wears a yellow robe and the other a robe of blue. About their necks are garlands of flowers and on their head coverings, floral wreaths. They are Prince Rama and his brother, Lakshman.

The eyes of all turn in adoration to the two princely heroes and follow them as they alight and walk barefooted around the arena, clockwise, before seating themselves upon a white cloth spread out for them. Though everyone in the crowd knows the names of the boys and their parents' occupations, at this time they see only the most beloved Hindu character, Rama, the mere utterance of whose name brings good fortune, and his brother, Lakshman, adored for his ever-remembered devotion to Rama.

An aged priest signals the beginning of the first scene of the Ram Lila, which often starts with the story of how Prince Rama's beautiful wife, Sita, was abducted by King Ravan.

Every morning, for nine days following, great battle scenes in the war between Prince Rama and King Ravan are presented. These culminate in a tense moment when King Ravan and his brother Kumbhakarna, represented by the immense effigies, are placed on a platform and blown up with fireworks. All those assembled, actors and onlookers, shout with exultation:

"Victory to Rama! Victory to Rama! Victory to Rama!"

The Drama of Rama, the Ram Lila, is presented differently in different parts of India, the lavishness of the performance depending on the size and wealth of the community. A friendly rivalry exists between neighboring villages and towns as to which will put on the pageant with greater pomp, a richer display of costumes, finer music, and more fireworks. But everywhere, once the pageant is begun, the audience listens with rapt attention, as if they had never before heard the story of the Adventures of Rama. Yet, should an actor stumble over any phrase, almost anyone in the audience, however young, could correct him. For not only are a number of episodes in the story of Prince Rama acted out each year during the festival, but from early childhood every boy frequently hears the story from his father; and every girl hears it from her mother or grandmother. For no other story is more popular in India than The Adventures of Rama, called the Ramayan or Ramayana.

The Ramayana is better known and better loved by the people of India than any other work in their vast literature. Even though to the Hindus Prince Rama is the incarnation of their God Vishnu, and Princess Sita the daughter of the goddess Mother

Earth, the people love Rama and Sita for their nobility as human beings. Rama is regarded with greater awe and respect, but Sita is most beloved. Her beauty, her courage, her devotion, her dignity in adversity, and above all her tenderness and kindliness, make her the queen of every Hindu heart.

During the ten-day festival dedicated to the Divine Mother, the people of India joyfully recall the Golden Age, a thousand times a thousand years ago and more, and they re-enact events in the adventurous lives of their beloved Rama and Sita in the Drama of Rama, based on the Ramayana.

Other Books on the Same Topic

THOSE wishing to understand the significance of the Ramayana to the people who produced it, and its place in world literature, will find it helpful to have a general view of India's culture before and during the times in which the Ramayana was produced, revised and accepted.

Following are a few works obtainable in most libraries. These books supply the general background of the historical origins of the epic and the reasons for its having so completely captivated the people of India from generation to generation over a great number of centuries.

INDIA: A SHORT CULTURAL HISTORY, by H. G. Rawlinson; Appleton-Century, New York, 1938.

A large but very interesting volume which presents India's culture in terms of its geography and history covering the prehistoric period to the twentieth century. This book treats religion, art and literature and shows their interrelation. It is particularly valuable in clarifying why the Hindus have such love and reverence for Rama, the hero of the Ramayana, and how this love and reverence express themselves in Hindu art to the present day.

THE DAWN OF LITERATURE, by Carl Holliday; Thomas Y. Crowell, New York, 1931.

This compact introduction to the earliest literatures of the world, that arose in Egypt, Assyria, Babylonia, Persia, China and Palestine, also contains an excellent chapter on India, dealing with India's religious, epic and lyric literature. The Ramayana and the Mahabharata are briefly but perceptively discussed.

A HISTORY OF INDIAN LITERATURE, by Herbert H. Cowen; Appleton, New York, 1931.

This delightful one-volume introduction to the vast field of Hindu literature, from the Vedas to the present day, devotes four chapters to the "Great Epics," of interest to the reader of the Ramayana. The book contains a good bibliography for further exploration.

THE GREAT INDIAN EPICS, by John Campbell Oman; George Bell & Sons, London, 1894.

A summary, in prose, of the two great Hindu epics, the Ramayana and the Mahabharata, with notes and illustrations, by an Englishman who lived in India and made Indian life a major concern of his inquiries. An old book, but still the best of its kind in this field.

HINDU LITERATURE, or, THE ANCIENT BOOKS OF INDIA, by Elizabeth A. Reed; Griggs & Co., Chicago, 1891.

Four chapters of this book are devoted to the Ramayana, beginning with a discussion of the age of the work, its authorship, the historical basis of the story, and the two main versions. Underscored are the similarities and differences between the Ramayana and the Greek epic, the Iliad, contrasting Helen of Troy with Princess Sita. The book devotes over a hundred pages to the story of this epic in prose, with a number of quotations in verse, taken principally from the translations of Ralph Griffith and Sir Monier Monier-Williams.

THE RAMAYANA AND THE MAHABHA-RATA, by Romesh C. Dutt; Dutton, New York, 1900.

In the first part of this volume (obtainable in Everyman's Library edition) the twenty-four thousand verses of Valmiki's Ramayana are presented in two thousand modern verses by the Hindu poet and scholar who attempts to preserve in his own version the rich imagery and descriptive parts of the epic. The verses are followed by an essay on the Ramayana, its poetic form, its uninterrupted fascination to the Hindu mind through successive generations, and why one must know this epic (along with the Mahabharata) if one wishes to understand the people of India.

THE RAMÁYÁN BY VALMIKI, translated into English verse by Ralph T. H. Griffith (five volumes); Trubner & Co., London, 1870-1874.

This is an almost complete, and most remarkable, translation of the first six books of the Ramayana into English couplets. Wherever sections are omitted, Griffith gives a digest of the material left out and the reason for the omission. The seventh book of the epic he presents in prose, basing himself mainly on the Italian prose translation by Gorresio — the first translation of the epic into a European language. If all the versions of the Ramayana (in Sanskrit, Prakrit, Hindi, Tamil, Bengali, or other languages of India) were lost, it would be possible to reconstruct a Hindu version of the epic from the work accomplished by Griffith in his magnificent translation.

(There are two other complete translations of *The Ramayana by Valmiki* in English: one, a literal translation in seven volumes by Pratap Chandra Roy; and another, in five volumes, by Babu Manmatha Nath Dutt. These are, however, difficult to obtain in most libraries.)

RAMACARITAMANASA, by Goswami Tulasi Das; translated by W. D. P. Hill; Oxford, New York, 1952.

For anyone who wishes to compare the Valmiki version with that of Tulasi Das (also known as Tulsi-Das or Tulasidas), the Hill translation is the most easily available and considered by some scholars as very good. (There exists another and excellent translation of this work, with fine illustrations in color, but it is not so easily obtained, for it appeared in the magazine *Kalyana Kalpataru* in three long installments, during August 1949, August 1950 and August 1951.)

THE TALES AND TEACHINGS OF HINDU-ISM, by D. S. Sarma; Hinds Kitabs Ltd., Bombay, 1948.

This small book by a principal of a college in Madras, India, is a delightful introduction to the lore and literature of Hinduism, including compact summaries of the two great epics. The writer has a lively mind, a fine sense of humor, and a lucid pen. He writes as one of our times for people of our times. The great regret is that this book, and others from his pen, are not easily available.

MYTHS AND LEGENDS OF INDIA, by J. M. Macfie; T. & T. Clark, Edinburgh, 1924.

A good collection of legends selected from the sacred books of India. Chapters 20-23 are taken from the Ramayana and deal with "Vishnu's Incarnation as

Rama," "Rama's Loyalty to Truth," "Rama and Sita," and "Rama's Ascent to Heaven."

RAMA, THE HERO OF INDIA, by Dhan Gopal Mukerji; Dutton, New York, 1930.

A prose and fictionized version of *The Ramayana by Valmiki* presented reverently by the well-known Hindu writer, for younger readers. Contains interesting illustrations.

THE MASTER MONKEY, by Dhan Gopal Mukerji; Dutton, New York, 1932.

The story of Hanuman, the monkey-god and patron saint of athletics in India. The first part of the book tells the story of Hanuman's divine origin and his adventures before he becomes involved in the search for Sita; the second part follows the Ramayana story, given entirely from Hanuman's point of view.

QUEST FOR SITA, by Maurice Collings; An Asia Book, John Day, New York, 1947.

This is a romantic tale about a Chinese girl named Swallow, who meets a Sage named Wu Shan. The Sage turns out to be an incarnation of Rama; and when he puts Swallow into a trance, she discovers that in a past incarnation she was Sita. What Swallow experiences in her trance is a highly fictionized recital of Sita's abduction and her trials in King Ravan's court, as given in the Ramayana.

Index

NOTE ON NAMES: We are not often confused by names in our own language, no matter how similar they may sound. But similar-sounding names in other languages perplex us. This is particularly true of many Hindu names encountered by the reader for the first time. Each Hindu name has a distinct meaning, and that meaning can be changed by the change of a single letter. An easily overlooked change of one vowel in a long Hindu name may make it the name of the king, or the queen, of a country rather than the name of the country itself. Also, proper names of both men and women frequently end with *a*, which to us tends to make them seem to belong to the same gender — Rama, Sita, Satrughna, Bharata, Lakshmana, etc. To add to the confusion, the names are spelled differently in different versions of the same story and in different Hindu dialects.

In the attempt to make the names in this book stand out distinctly to the Western reader, proper names have not always been presented in accordance with the Sanskrit version of Valmiki. In some names the final *a* has been dropped, just as it has been dropped in certain versions. For the reader who may still lose his bearings, all important characters and place names in the epic are identified in the following Index by their relationship in the story.